HALF LOVE

***First Episode of the Series* Divyotsav**

By Vinny Streak

AF673205

"One sided lover is a snail walking on a blade where going forward hurts, Going backwards hurts more and being still on the same place will cut that in half. What should be the exact time to make it two sided before it gets too late"

@vinny.streak

2026

Half Love

Published by: Vinny Streak

First Edition: February 2026

ISBN: 978-93-5777-797-1

Printed in India

Disclaimer

"Lord Krishna was known as *Madhusudan* because he slew a demon, and *Govinda* because he loved the cows. His names were not his identity; his deeds were."

In this story, the names **Utsav**, **Aditi**, **Shyam**, or **Chronos** are merely borrowed labels. They are empty vessels waiting for your memories to fill them.

- **If reading this reminds you of a backbencher who saved you a seat:** Then this is not the story of Utsav; it is the story of your best friend.
- **If the corridors of Vidya International feel familiar:** Then this is not a fictional school in a fictional city; it is the geography of your own childhood.
- **If you see a heartbreak:** Then this is a tragedy.
- **If you see a sacrifice:** Then this is a love story.

This book is not a public commentary; it is a private mirror. The story not only belongs to the writer. It belongs to the eyes that are reading it. **"Yatha Drishti, Tatha Srishti."** (As is your vision, so is the world).

Welcome to **Your** Story.

Index :-

CHAPTER -1

The Silent Decade

Sumit had been in a relationship with Aarohi for ten years, but she only found out about it today.

To the rest of the world, he was just a boy growing up, studying B. Com, and struggling with exams. But inside his head, he was never alone. He had created an exact replica, a perfect shadow of a girl he saw once from a guava tree, and she raised him throughout those ten years. She taught him how to dress, how to speak, and how to be loyal.

One pleasant day in November 2023, he finally found her Instagram profile. After searching through mutual contacts, he stared at the 'Follow' button. He wasn't just adding a friend; he was introducing himself to the woman who had been his full-time imaginary companion for a decade.

The room was cold with that specific November chill. His phone battery sat at 14%, but he couldn't bring himself to get the charger. His thumb hovered over the blue button.

Follow. Six letters. A request. But it felt like the trigger of a loaded gun.

He looked at her small profile picture. She was looking away, smiling. She looked different from the nine-year-old girl he remembered. The baby fat was gone, replaced by the sharp elegance of adulthood. But her hair still cascaded down one shoulder, just like it had in 2013.

He took a deep breath. Outside, a stray dog barked. Inside, his heart hammered a frantic rhythm.

Do it, Sumit. You are not a child anymore.

He closed his eyes. He didn't see the dark; he saw the Section B classroom. He saw dust floating in the sunlight. He saw Aditi's braid swinging. And he felt the crushing weight of the words Utsav never said to her. The silence that had cost him everything.

He opened his eyes. The blue button was waiting.

If he didn't press it, he would remain safe. He could keep the Imaginary Aarohi—the one who never argued, who loved him unconditionally, who always knew what to say.

But if he pressed it, he risked everything. What if the real Aarohi was cruel? Boring? Taken? What if she didn't remember him, or the guava tree?

Real life is messy. Imagination is clean. Utsav had chosen safety and lived with regret.

"Not in my case," he whispered.

He pressed his thumb down. The button turned gray. *Requested.*

Breath rushed out of him. He tossed the phone onto the bed and stared at the ceiling fan. The veil between his ten-year dream and reality had lifted. Now, he waited.

For the next forty-eight hours, his life shrank to a 6-inch screen. The button remained gray. It was purgatory.

He checked his phone every seven minutes, swiping to refresh, seeing nothing but reels of cats and cars.

The Imaginary Aarohi became quiet. For the first time in a decade, he couldn't hear her voice. It was as if she was packing her bags, making space for the reality about to crash into him.

"Why hasn't she accepted?" he asked the ceiling on the second night.

He walked a tightrope of anxiety. If she deleted the request, he would have to go back to being Utsav—the boy who stood in silence.

On the morning of the third day, a sharp buzz vibrated.

@aaroheyyyy_ accepted your follow request. @aaroheyyyy_ started following you.

The air left his lungs. She had followed back. He sat on the edge of his bed, feeling a heavy, warm relief settle into his bones. The ten-year wait was over.

They didn't speak immediately. For the first few weeks, they existed in the silent language of the "Story View." He would post a photo, and she would view it. She would post a sunset, and he would tap the "Like" heart. It was a digital dance, two satellites terrified to make contact. He was scared a simple "Hello" would break the spell. He needed a bridge.

Two months passed in this story era, filled with reactions and one-word remarks.

Then, on a Thursday evening, he posted a video tribute to Spider-Man 2—the Tobey Maguire era, focusing on sacrifice. The caption read: *"With great power comes great responsibility."*

Ten minutes passed. Twenty.

Ting.

It was a message from Aarohi. A full sentence. "This scene always makes him cry. Best Spider-Man ever."

His fingers hovered. The silence was broken. The replica was gone; the real Aarohi had arrived.

"The train scene? Yeah. It’s the definition of a hero," he typed, his heart hammering.

She is typing...

"Exactly," she replied. "Everyone loves the action, but I love how human he is. He struggles with his rent, his studies, his love life. He's not perfect."

Sumit smiled. The real Aarohi was deeper than the shadow, who never had opinions on superhero morality.

"He's relatable," he replied. "Maybe that's why they watch him. To see someone struggle and still choose to be good."

For the next forty-five minutes, the outside world ceased to exist. They didn't do the awkward "How are you?" routine. They dove straight into deep nostalgia, movies, and ideologies.

The timestamps blurred. There was no waiting three hours to reply to look cool. It was a flood. Ten years of unsaid words poured out through a conversation about a guy in a red mask. For forty-five minutes, he wasn't the boy from the guava tree, and he wasn't a stranger. They were just Sumit and Aarohi, discovering their frequencies matched.

When she finally sent, "I have to go, dad is calling," he put the phone down and closed his eyes. For the first time in ten years, he didn't miss the imaginary girl. The real one was so much better.

That night was a catalyst. The dam broke. They archived their lives for each other, moving from superheroes to dissecting college struggles, debating food choices, and drifting into heavy waters of spirituality. It felt like two old souls meeting again.

He learned the Imaginary Aarohi was a two-dimensional sketch. The Real Aarohi was a full-color painting. She was sharper, funnier, and more profound.

But with this intensity came a new fear. Every time a conversation ended, there was a pang of loss.

One night, she stopped abruptly.

"Sumit, I have to go. Dad is asking for me. Sorry. Bye. And sorry again." "Sorry for what?" he typed back. "Sorry if the bye hurts. I hate cutting it off."

He paused. To her, "Bye" felt like a door slamming shut. He thought about Utsav, who never got a "Bye" from Aditi, only an ending silence.

"Aarohi, listen to me. Byes don't hurt," he typed slowly. "A 'Bye' is a promise. It means 'I am going, but I will come back.' It's hopeful."

He took a breath. "Goodbyes hurt. 'Goodbye' means the story is over. You and I? We are just turning the page. So never apologize for a bye."

She sent a heart reaction. "Okay then. No goodbyes. Just bye."

He realized something thrilling. The imaginary girl had been perfect and safe. But the real girl cared about the difference between leaving and leaving forever. He didn't want the replica back. Reality was infinitely more precious.

To an outsider, they were just two friends catching up. But a ten percent gap—a frosted glass wall of "stranger-ness"—stood between them. While ninety percent of their connection flowed easily, that ten percent was a fortress where Sumit hid his soul.

To Aarohi, Sumit was a seven-month-old acquaintance. She didn't know the nine-year-old boy who had hung upside down from a guava tree just to glimpse her. She didn't know he had collected seconds of her presence to survive her absence. For ten years, he had dragged her shadow through high school and into his office cubicle.

He was terrified to bridge that gap. Confession could cut the veil, but it could also sever the thread. If he told her he had loved her before knowing what love meant, she might see it as obsession and run. So, he swallowed the ten years and locked the boy in a closet.

He made peace with the inequality. It was enough that the universe had aligned their coordinates. He was content to be an asteroid that had finally drifted close enough to feel her gravity.

But destiny had a plan. Sumit couldn't live with the regret of unexpressed love, nor did he want to ruin their seven months of comfort.

It started with a movie dialogue. He was watching *Ae Dil Hai Mushkil*, where Shah Rukh Khan explains the weight of unrequited love: *"The power of one-sided love is something else... unlike other relationships, it doesn't get divided between two people. Only I have the right to it."*

The words hit him like a physical blow. That was his last ten years. He owned his love for her. Impulsively, he shared the reel on his story. No caption.

Five minutes later. *Ting.*

"Who is this for?" Aarohi replied.

His heart stopped, then restarted at double speed. A direct demand for a name. Panicking, he spent thirty minutes hiding.

"It's just a movie scene. Why do you ask?" he typed, beating around the bush.

But she was sharp. She knew men don't post poetry about one-sided love without a muse.

"Sumit, stop dodging. Who is the girl?"

He stared at the glass. He could lie. But looking at her username, he realized he was tired of hiding. He wanted the light.

Taking a rattling breath, he typed the truth, wrapped in a riddle. "If you really want to see the girl, put your phone down and go stand in front of a mirror. You'll see her."

Sent.

The silence was deafening. The "seen" checkmark mocked him. Minutes ticked by. He felt sick, convinced he had crossed the line into creepy.

Then, it buzzed.

"Meet me. Starbucks. The one near the circle. Now."

She didn't wait for a yes. The drive was a blur. He reached the quiet, high-street Starbucks at 9:48 AM, ordered nothing, and watched the glass door.

Every time it chimed, he jumped. *Run before she rejects you!* the Utsav inside him screamed. But the Sumit who had loved her for a decade stayed.

At 9:55 AM, the door pushed open.

Seeing her in 3D was a shock. Photos didn't capture how she tucked a loose strand of hair behind her ear. She was real flesh and blood. Her eyes found him. Unsmiling, she walked straight to his table and pulled out a chair with a loud scrape.

"So," she said, her voice steady. "I'm the mirror girl?"

The coffee machine hissed. She leaned back, studying his face.

"I don't get it," she said slowly. "I used to think that because our fathers are friends, we were just inheriting a friendship. But one fine day, I get to know that you are in that much amount of love with me? That you've been loving me one-sidedly while I just thought we were sharing memes?"

He looked away. "I never wanted to share my feelings with you, Aarohi. I knew the moment you knew the truth, the friendship would become awkward. I didn't want to lose the little access I had to you."

She tilted her head. "Maybe. Or maybe you just assumed it would be awkward. Is that why you were beating around the bush about the 'Mirror Girl'?"

"I didn't want my words to hurt you," he said quickly, desperate for her to understand it was protection, not cowardice. "To be honest, I was happier before I followed you."

Aarohi blinked. "Excuse me?"

The dam broke. Ten years of monologue spilled into the Starbucks air.

"I was happier because in those days, she was with me. Your imagination... she was with me every single day. She was pure emotion. But ever since I clicked that button... she is gone. Reality scared her away."

The silence wasn't awkward; it was stunned.

"Wait," Aarohi held up a hand. "What? Imagination? You said 'she' was with you?"

His stomach dropped. He had admitted to the hallucination out loud.

"Ooooppps," he breathed out, squeezing his eyes shut. "I was just blabbering. Forget I said that."

"No," she said firmly. "I'm not forgetting that. Who was with you, Sumit?"

He cleared his throat awkwardly. "Okay. I know how this sounds. But please, don't think of her as a ghost. She didn't scare me. She was pure feeling. She was the best part of mine."

Aarohi frowned, stirring her iced coffee. "So, you're saying... I was there? Physically?"

"No," he said quickly. "But in every other way that mattered. Every time I felt alone, she was there. When I got low marks in a 9th-grade math test? You were the one who told me it wasn't the end of the world."

"I did?" Aarohi raised an eyebrow. "I hate math. I probably would have told you to burn the textbook."

He smiled weakly. "The real you, maybe. But the Imaginary You was patient. She said all those things I desperately wanted to hear but no one else was saying. We grew up together, Aarohi. People saw Sumit going to school, going to college, writing exams. But inside? It was me and your Imagination, growing up side by side."

Aarohi stopped stirring, looking at him with a mix of fascination and skepticism. "You talked to her? Like... conversations?"

"Constantly," he admitted. "As I got older, my problems got bigger. I didn't know what to do with my life, what to write, how to be a man. She helped me. She never left me alone. There were times I could have gone down a bad path. Easy mistakes. But I didn't, because I couldn't face her if I did. She forced me to be a better person."

He met her eyes. "I'm who I am today because she sculpted me. She made me so great that I was ready for you."

Aarohi remained silent, trying to process this massive, invisible reality.

"So," she said slowly, "you built a version of me to keep yourself good?"

"I didn't build her," he corrected gently. "I just... kept her. From the moment I first saw you. It wasn't gradual, Aarohi. When I saw you the first time... it was instant. It was love at first sight."

The air shifted. Her softness vanished, replaced by a sharp crease between her eyebrows. She looked more confused than she had about the imagination part.

"Love at first sight?" she repeated, her voice rising slightly. "Sumit, you followed me on Instagram in November. We've been talking for 11 months. You fell in love with my profile picture?" She shook her head, looking almost offended. "That's not love. That's just liking a photo. You can't claim 'Love at First Sight' from a digital screen."

He realized he had skipped a chapter. She didn't know the story began in 2013.

"No. Not the screen," Sumit shook his head slowly. "You think the first time I saw you was on a 6-inch display? The first time I saw you, I was twenty feet in the air, hanging upside down like a bat in a school uniform."

Aarohi choked on her iced coffee. She coughed, laughing and wiping her mouth. "Wait. Pause. A bat? In a school uniform?"

"It was 2013," Sumit explained, drifting into his storytelling cadence. "I was in my courtyard. We had this rebel guava tree that gave fruit in all three seasons."

"So, you were attacking this magical tree?" she smirked, leaning her chin on her palm.

"I was harvesting," he corrected. "I was twenty feet high. I had locked my knees over my favorite branch, body dangling down, blood rushing to my head, eating a guava. And that's when you walked in."

Her smile faded slightly. "Me? In 2013?"

"Yes. You had come along when your father visited mine. You stopped near the boundary wall, about thirty feet away."

"I remember that wall," Aarohi blinked.

"You stood there and asked in your sweet voice, 'Uncle? Is anyone home?'" Sumit leaned across the table. "I was directly above, but thirty feet is a long distance when you are upside down. I wanted to see the face that matched that sweet voice. I reached out, gripped the rough bark with just my right arm, took a breath, and slowly unhooked my knees."

"Wait, you didn't just jump down? You swung?"

"It wasn't a slide; it was a pivot," Sumit mimicked the action. "Gravity snatched me. My entire body weight snapped down, held only by my right arm. I swung out, spinning in mid-air from upside-down to right-side-up. It was a blur. And precisely in the middle of that spin... my eyes found you."

"Across the thirty feet?" she asked softly.

"Across the thirty feet. The world was spinning, but you stood perfectly still. I only remember your face because nothing else mattered. Your beautiful, deep ocean-like eyes. The direct sunlight on your cheeks. Your eyebrows sharp as swords. Your short, rosy lips. Your long, silky hair that made the night seem dark."

Aarohi stared at him, baffled. "My God! You are crazy. Let me get this straight. You fell in love with me while spinning in mid-air? Holding on with one arm?"

"Exactly."

"Sumit," she laughed softly. "Did the wind blow? Did violins play?"

"In my head? A whole orchestra," Sumit smiled nostalgically. "But outside, I just hurried to climb down and talk to you. When I fell in love with you, I only saw your face. I kept falling. In a few days, it peaked to a level where I started seeing you in my dreams."

She shook her head, a blush creeping up her neck. She tried to make it a joke, but felt the weight of it. "You're crazy. You remembered a five-second spin for ten years?"

"I didn't just remember it. I built a life around it."

Sumit took a sip of water, the cafe noise fading as he drifted back.

"That spin was just the prologue. After that day... you didn't just walk away. You went back to your world, a hundred kilometers away."

"Yeah. We only came to your city for summer vacations," Aarohi nodded slowly.

"To a nine-year-old boy, a hundred kilometers might as well be a different galaxy," Sumit said, his voice heavy with old frustration. "I became obsessed with the calendar. I waited for summer like a farmer waits for rain. Every time your father visited mine, I would hide behind the curtain, praying to see two figures walking in. But it was always just him."

Sumit turned back to her, the pain still sharp. "You were a 'blue moon' event, Aarohi. I thought I could wait for the next time. But seasons changed, and I never saw you. I was frustrated, angry, and hollow. Then, exactly thirteen months later, the dam broke. Not because you visited, but because I realized I couldn't survive the distance."

"So... you gave up?" Aarohi frowned.

"No," Sumit whispered. "I adapted. I realized if reality wouldn't bring you here, I had to bring you myself. God saw I was suffering. He couldn't send the real you, so He sent me a copy. He sent me Her."

"The Imagination," Aarohi realized.

"Yes. It happened in the thirteenth month. I was sitting alone on the terrace, feeling that familiar sadness. Suddenly... I didn't feel alone. I felt a presence. It was you. Not the girl far away, but a version that could stay." Sumit tapped his chest. "From that day on, the hundred kilometers didn't matter. I stopped watching the gate. I went through school, exams, and family drama talking to her. She became my diary and my conscience. When I say I've been with you for ten years, I'm not lying. I spent every single day talking to the soul God sent to keep me company."

Aarohi stared at him. She wasn't laughing anymore. She looked at him like he was a man who had survived a desert by hallucinating an oasis—only to find out the water was real.

"You really loved her," she whispered. "The imaginary me."

"I needed her. She wasn't just a daydream. She was a necessity. She kept my real life and my imaginary life balanced. She kept your face sharp in my mind and helped me control the uncontrollable love I had for you. It was too much energy for one boy to hold; she gave me a place to pour it."

"So, she was... therapy?" Aarohi asked, brow furrowed.

"She was a partner. That version of you made me the better version of myself. I finished school with her sitting beside me. I went to college, and she walked the hallways with me. For nine years, I asked her questions, and she answered."

"What kind of questions?"

"Everything," Sumit smiled. "From 'Should I study for this exam?' to 'Does she still remember me?' She always had the right answer."

Aarohi bit her lip, the romanticism warring with reality. "Sumit, I know you're making it sound poetic. But... doesn't it feel a bit... psycho? Talking to a girl who isn't there for nine years? Isn't that something a crazy person does?"

Sumit didn't flinch. He looked at her with calm certainty. "If loving you unconditionally is being psycho, then I am proudly a psycho."

Taken aback by his lack of shame, Aarohi shifted in her chair. "Okay. Let's say you aren't crazy. But what were your intentions? Visualizing me, talking to me... did you never plan to come to my city and make me yours?"

Sumit laughed, a dry, hollow sound. "Aarohi, listen to me closely. There is no possessiveness in my love. People think love is grabbing someone and saying, 'You are mine.' But if there are restrictions, it is a possession, not a relationship. Possession is a cage. You lock a bird in a cage because you love how it sings, but you forget that the bird sings best when it's flying."

He looked deep into her eyes. "You never get a girl. You can only be with her. I didn't want to own you. I just wanted to be with you. I was with you in my mind, so I was happy. I didn't need to 'get' you to love you."

Aarohi sat frozen, having expected a confession of obsession, but receiving a definition of freedom instead. Still, she wasn't letting him off the hook.

"That sounds noble," she crossed her arms. "But didn't it ever cross your mind that you were missing out? That you needed me here, in the flesh?"

"Need is a strong word," Sumit shook his head. "I wanted you, sure. But I didn't need you to survive. My love was self-sustaining."

"So, you had zero expectations? You never hoped I would love you back?"

"Never. Love is always without expectations. Otherwise, it becomes a barter system. An exchange. I wasn't looking to trade; I was just looking to give."

Aarohi processed the logic before shifting gears. "Okay, Mr. Philosopher. But practically... how did you talk to this 'Imaginary Aarohi'?"

"The way people usually talk. I spoke. She answered in my head. I spoke again."

"Out loud?" her eyes widened.

"Sometimes," he admitted. "When the emotion was strong."

She giggled, covering her mouth. "Sumit... you know how that looks, right? From a third-party perspective, it's just you talking to the wind. People would have considered you mentally unstable."

"Oh, they did," Sumit grinned. "In fact, they thought I was possessed."

"Tell me," Aarohi leaned forward, smiling.

"Back in college, there was this guy, Debashish Roy. One evening, I was sitting on the hostel bench, deep in passionate conversation with the imaginary you, waving my hands at empty space. Debashish watched me for ten minutes. He ran back terrified and told everyone Sumit was possessed."

Aarohi covered her mouth, shaking with silent laughter.

"Around midnight, I felt a strange heat," Sumit continued. "I opened my eyes and thought I had woken up in a cult. Nine guys in black clothes stood around my bed. On the floor, drawn in wheat flour and turmeric, were complex triangles. In the center was a dry animal bone."

"No way," Aarohi gasped.

"Yes way. They were chanting. Then Debashish stepped forward with a mug of water. He dipped his fingers in, sprinkled it on my face, and yelled, 'In the name of the Lord and the Holy Spirit, Jesus Christ, leave this body!'"

Aarohi snorted loudly.

"Exactly," Sumit said. "I sat up, wiped my face, and yelled: 'Debashish, you are a Bengali! Those are Tantric Black Magic artworks! You're standing like a pagan exorcism! And you are chanting Bible verses?! What is going on here?!'"

Aarohi threw her head back and laughed loudly, clutching her stomach. Sumit slammed his hand on the table, laughing at the memory.

"He mixed the religions?" she wheezed.

"He covered all the bases! He didn't know which ghost it was, so he used a buffet of exorcisms!"

They laughed until their sides hurt, dissolving the tension of the last ten years. For a moment, they were just two people roaring with laughter over an exorcism meant to cure a love that wasn't a disease.

As the laughter faded into a comfortable silence, Aarohi turned serious again.

"So, through half of school and all of college... haven't you met or seen any other girl? Did you really never prioritize anyone else?"

Sumit shook his head. "The unconditionally loving Aarohi made me loyal. I focused on my studies and writing. I didn't have time to look around because I was always looking in." He leaned back. "The irony of life is, when you aren't desperate, you get everything. Because I ignored everyone else, I got so many proposals. Girls liked that I wasn't chasing them. But I became the Master of the Friend Zone."

"Okay, so you had options. But you never desired to see what a relationship was like?"

Sumit’s face hardened. The playfulness vanished. "No. Relationships are traps."

"Traps? Why?"

Sumit sighed, seeing a ghost from college. "Because I saw what happened to Parth."

"Who is Parth?"

"My batchmate. Second-year Mechanical Engineering. A decent guy. He got into an intense relationship with a smart, stylish girl from BBA. He used to brag to us, 'Bro, her family is so supportive. They give us full freedom. Her parents even go out for walks to leave us alone at home.'"

Aarohi raised an eyebrow. "That sounds good."

"That’s what we thought. We thought he hit the jackpot. But one year later, Parth realized they weren't compatible. So, he refused to marry her. The next day, thirty-five cops approached the college gate."

"Thirty-five?" Aarohi gasped.

"Like they were coming for a terrorist. They grabbed Parth by his collar in front of the whole department and dragged him to the station. The girl and her 'supportive' family filed a case under the pretext of marriage and cheating. Every section they could throw."

Aarohi went silent.

"Parth survived one and a half years in prison," Sumit's voice was void of emotion. "A student, rotting in a cell because he thought 'freedom' was love. His family had to sell land and hand over seven lakhs as compensation."

"And then?" Aarohi whispered. "He broke up?"

Sumit looked her dead in the eye. "No. After prison, after the seven lakhs, after the humiliation... they married also."

"That is why I call it a trap, Aarohi. You walk in because the door is open, the parents are smiling, and the freedom is sweet. But the moment you try to leave, you realize the door only locks from the outside. I didn't want a trap. I wanted you. And since I couldn't have you in reality without risk... I kept you in my head. It was safer."

Aarohi leaned back, the laughter completely gone. She looked at him with a gaze analyzing his soul.

"So," she said slowly. "You love me. But you are not possessive. You are not protective. You offer freedom, and you place no obligation on me to love you back."

"Yes," Sumit nodded gently. "Love isn't a debt, Aarohi. You don't owe me anything."

She shook her head in frustration. "Why, Sumit? If you fell in love with me at first sight—from that guava tree—then why do you not want me as a person? Why don't you want to call me your girlfriend? I'm confused."

Sumit leaned forward, his voice dropping to a heavy whisper.

"Because I love you the way you are. I don't want to change you or bind you. The fact that God sent you into this world, breathing the same air, living under the same sky—that is enough."

He looked at her hands.

"I don't crave your attention; I crave your happiness. I want your desires to come true. Everything you dream of should come to your life. Even if none of those things include me."

Aarohi stayed silent, absorbing the sheer selflessness that went against every rule of modern dating.

"In what relation do you see me, then?" she asked finally. "If not a girlfriend, what?"

Sumit smiled peacefully.

"It is totally up to you, Aarohi. My love is not a bondage. Whatever relation you consider me in—I will perform it." He spread his hands. "If you want a friend, I will be the best friend. If you want a guide, I will be your compass. If you want a stranger who watches from afar, I will be that stranger. And if you do not want to name it... I will be the 'Unnamed' in your life."

He paused, looking into her eyes. The poet who had written to her shadow for ten years finally spoke to the reality.

"You ask what I want? I want nothing. Because frankly, Aarohi, I already feel inferior."

"Inferior?" she asked. "To whom?"

"To the things that get to touch you without asking," Sumit said softly. "I feel inferior to the mirror that sees your face every morning. I feel jealous of the comb that runs through your hair. I envy the glass of water that touches your lips. I am jealous of the wind that holds you outside. I envy the pillow that holds your dreams every night. And I feel inferior to the sun, which has the privilege of waking you up."

His voice trembled slightly.

"If you are simply existing, that is the ultimate happiness for me. Seeing you happy, seeing your achievements... that makes my day. I don't need to be the cause of your smile, Aarohi. I just need to know you are smiling."

The cafe seemed to disappear. Aarohi didn't blink, her eyes shimmering with tears of awe.

"The mother who raised you..." she whispered. "She must be so great. She taught you love is about giving, not taking. She raised a gentleman in a world full of players. I don't know if I deserve this kind of love, Sumit... but the woman who made you this way deserves a salute."

Aarohi leaned across the table, her eyes twinkling with her trademark mischief.

"Okay, Sumit," she tapped her straw. "Since you've spent ten years perfecting the 'Imaginary Aarohi,' I'm at a disadvantage. I've only known the 'Real Sumit' for forty-five minutes of chat and twenty minutes of coffee. Tell me something about the real you that the imaginary me would never have guessed."

Sumit shifted, a playful smirk tugging his lips. "Well, the imaginary she was much more polite about my school uniform. She never once called me a bat."

"Because she was trapped in your head!" Aarohi laughed. "She was a captive audience! She probably wanted to tell you hanging upside down in green pants is a fashion crime, but she didn't want to hurt your feelings. Now, tell me the truth. Do you still have the guava tree instinct? If I pointed at that decorative plant, would you pivot off the espresso machine to reach it?"

"The espresso machine is too low," Sumit replied with mock seriousness. "The angle for centrifugal force would be all wrong. I'd end up in the pastry display."

Aarohi snorted. "The 'Mirror Girl' would record it for her story while the barista calls security. But seriously, Sumit, you friend-zoned everyone in college to be 'loyal' to a shadow. Doesn't that make you a heartbreaker? Is there a support group for girls rejected by a guy 'married' to his imagination?"

"I wouldn't call it a support group," Sumit joked. "Maybe just a confused WhatsApp group. But I told them I wasn't looking for a relationship! I just didn't tell them it was because I was debating life philosophy with a girl who lived a hundred kilometers away and didn't know I existed."

"And the 'Real Me' is passing the test?" she teased. "Or are you thinking the imaginary one was quieter and didn't ask annoying questions?"

Sumit looked at her, the humor in his eyes softening. "The imaginary you was a sketch, Aarohi. A beautiful one, but just lines on a page. You? You're in 3D. You make fun of me, and you drink coffee too fast. The imaginary you never had a caffeine crash. You probably will. And honestly? I prefer the crash. It's more human."

"Oh, so you like flaws?" Aarohi challenged. "What if I told you I think Spider-Man 3 is the best one because of the emo dance scene?"

Sumit recoiled in theatrical horror. "We have to draw the line somewhere. If you defend the emo dance, I might have to call Debashish Roy back for a real exorcism."

"Hey! It was iconic!" she defended, laughing. She reached out, lightly tapping his hand. "You're a weird guy, Sumit. But I think the mirror has been lucky to see you every day too."

Sumit felt the familiar hammer in his chest, but he didn't need to imagine her response. It was right there, smiling back.

The laughter settled into a charged silence. Aarohi stirred her drink.

"Sumit," her voice dropped into a more intimate register. "You've spent ten years with a version of me. I want to know the feeling. What do you feel right now, seeing me in person, compared to that imaginary world?"

He looked at her, finally seeing the sun after a long dream of light.

"In the imaginary world, you were a finished masterpiece. You were constant. It was like listening to my favorite song on repeat—perfect, mine, and unchanging. A love of certainty." He leaned in. "But seeing you here? It's a love of discovery. In my head, I couldn't smell your vanilla and rain perfume. I couldn't see your left eyebrow hitch when you disagree. I couldn't hear the resonance of your laugh."

Aarohi smiled shyly. "So, the imaginary me was a robot?"

"No. She was an angel. But angels don't have flaws or surprises. Sitting here, I feel a sense of gravity. When I was with her, I was in control. But with you? I have no control. You could say something that ruins my week, or something that makes me feel like I'm back in that tree."

"Is that scary? Losing control?"

"It's terrifying," Sumit admitted. "But it's the most alive I've felt in a decade. The imaginary world was a sanctuary, but this is a revolution. In the imaginary world, I loved a concept of you. In the real world, I am falling in love with the fact of you. The fact that you are entirely separate from my mind." He paused. "The imaginary Aarohi was a beautiful lie I told myself to survive the silence. But the real you is a truth I never thought I'd be lucky enough to hear."

Aarohi reached across, brushing his sleeve. "You're still a poet, Sumit. But I prefer being a 'truth' over a 'concept'."

Aarohi broke the silence later, her voice raspy. "Sumit, it's one o'clock. We've been here three hours. You've told me you love me." She hesitated, nervously twisting a napkin. Underneath her confusion, a secret burned—a love for someone else she hadn't dared mention. She felt guilty, yet desperate for a way out. "Where does this leave us? Are you asking me to be your girlfriend?"

Sumit didn't blink. He gave her a surrendered smile.

"I don't want to be your boyfriend, Aarohi. If I call you 'mine,' I am creating a cage. I saw what cages do to people. I don't want to own you. I want to love you."

Aarohi felt a sharp, dizzying relief. Her secret stayed safe. "A friend? You just want to be friends?"

"I want us to be the kind of friends the world doesn't have a label for. I want to be your constant. I want you to be free to love whoever you want. If I 'get' you, the story ends. If we are friends, I get to keep your existence in my world forever. You stay free."

Aarohi looked away, her heart hammering. She felt like a fraud, yet mesmerized by his selflessness. She accepted the "Friendzone" as a sanctuary to keep him close without confessing her own heart.

"You're a beautiful, selfless psycho, Sumit," she laughed softly. "Most guys would demand a 'yes' or 'no'. You're handing me a 'forever' with no strings attached."

"I crave your happiness, not your possession," Sumit smiled. "The boy from the guava tree doesn't need to hold your hand to walk beside you."

Aarohi touched his hand affectionately, accepting the peace between her reality and his imagination.

"Okay, Sumit," she whispered. "No labels. No cages. Just us. The Mirror Girl and the Boy from the Tree."

She smiled, but her eyes remained guarded with her untold secret. Sumit didn't notice the shadow; he was just happy he didn't have to talk to the air to be heard.

The 1:00 PM rush transformed Starbucks. The quiet air was gone, replaced by roasted beans, clacking keyboards, and corporate drone. College couples laughed nearby.

The silence between them had shifted from the ache of a boy chasing a ghost to the settled peace of two people on the same shore. Arohi felt profound relief. The expectation to be his perfect "girlfriend" was gone. She wasn't his deity; she was herself.

Across from her, Sumit felt a joy bordering on spiritual. The imaginary had become flesh and blood. He could simply speak, and she would hear him. The agonizing distance had collapsed into this shared table. They were finally something real. They were friends.

Suddenly, Arohi's expression clouded with jagged confusion. She looked at him like a riddle. The clarity vanished, replaced by a clawing question.

Sumit noticed instantly. A knowing smirk played on his lips.

"Any more questions, Sherlock Holmes?" he asked lightly.

Arohi didn't smile. She locked her gaze on his. "Probably, yes. I want to ask... if you were so happy with your imagination, why?

You knew I couldn't be yours. You knew my limitations. If you never wanted to disrupt that perfect world, why did you choose to express all of this to me now?"

The cafe noise faded to a dull hum. Sumit looked down, then back at her, his expression stripped of pretense.

"Because, Arohi, even the most beautiful ghost eventually starts to feel like a haunting," he breathed. "I worshiped the version of you I created because it was safe. But I told you because I was tired of being the only person who knew you existed. I didn't tell you so I could 'have' you. I told you so that for once, the girl in my head and the girl in the world could finally meet. I had to let the imagination die so that you and I could finally start to live—even if 'living' just means sitting here as friends."

Arohi's brow furrowed. "I want to know the fact. Why express these feelings now?"

Sumit leaned back, the smirk fading. "Because," he said quietly, "I didn't want to repeat the same mistake Utsav did to Aditi."

Arohi paused. "Who is Utsav? And what happened to him?"

"It's a very long story," Sumit sighed. "And I think rich people like you have a bit of a time shortage."

Arohi scoffed playfully. "Why are you mocking me? I'm just a college student on vacation. I'm free until 7 PM. Tell me. I want to see what made you eager to break this ten-year cage."

Sumit looked out the window. "It's the story of someone who believed love didn't need words. He thought his efforts and deeds would do the talking."

"I get the helicopter view," Arohi murmured. "Tell me about Utsav and Aditi."

Sumit took a breath, and the modern walls of Starbucks dissolved, replaced by the dusty corridors of a school years ago.

It is a beautiful case of a one-sided lover of Vidya International School, Vijay Chowk, Chronicle, Chronos.

CHAPTER -2

693: The Cost of a Crown

In the sanctuary of discipline that was Section 3-A, the air smelled of sharpened pencils and high expectations. At the peak of its hierarchy sat Anshu—a prodigy whose terrifying intelligence often surpassed seniors in the eighth grade. She was the sun around which the school's academic solar system revolved.

Orbiting close behind was Utsav. He was the perpetual "Silver Boy," the model student with perfectly tucked shirts and finished homework, living a life of structured ambition.

But destiny disrupted the order, disguised as a missing duster.

While 3-A sat in its semi-quiet rhythm, Utsav was sent to the section next door, Class 3-B, to retrieve their duster.

He left the monastery of 3-A and walked into the coliseum of 3-B.

The noise hit him like a physical wave. Boys vaulted over desks; chalk flew like grenades. It was a kingdom of unrestrained energy. Scanning the room for the duster, his orderly mind calculated the chaos.

And then, his eyes found the only thing that wasn't moving.

Aditi.

Sitting in the middle row, she was entirely in her own world, revising the fourth period's lesson untouched by the madness. As a topper himself, Utsav immediately recognized her as one too.

She possessed a translucent, porcelain complexion that glowed against the dull classroom. Her delicate face held soft cheekbones and naturally pale rose lips. Her wide, almond-shaped eyes were mesmerizing—brown pools of uncorrupted sincerity, brimming with a purity the world hadn't yet tarnished. She looked like a prayer in a room full of noise.

But framing this ethereal face was the feature that bound Utsav's soul to the doorway.

Her hair.

It was a living waterfall of midnight. Long, thick, and silken, it defied gravity, tumbling past her waist to rest gently against her thighs. It shimmered with every movement, a dark halo protecting her from the noise.

Utsav, the boy who memorized textbooks and chased marks, felt his mind go blank. The crushing dominance of Anshu's grades was forgotten. He stood frozen. He had come for a blackboard tool but found himself staring at a girl who had wiped his mind clean. In that innocent perfection, Utsav realized he had never truly seen anything beautiful until this moment.

Utsav had always been a boy of retention. But after that day, his memory became a sieve. He forgot his lunchbox, his shoelaces, and that the Earth revolved around the Sun.

Because Utsav had found a new face.

It was the only thing his mind refused to delete. He became a desperate pilgrim hunting for glimpses of his shrine in the school corridors. Seeing her wasn't a want; it was a biological necessity. And since he couldn't just walk into 3-B and stare, he invented ridiculous, pathetic excuses to cross into enemy territory.

The Case of the "Invisible" Red Chalk

One Wednesday, Utsav convinced himself his Math teacher desperately needed red chalk. He marched into 3-B, only to find Mrs. Suman—the strictest teacher in the junior wing—eyeing him like a hawk.

"What do you want, Section A?" she snapped.

"Chalk, Ma'am. Red chalk. For... important geometry."

"Important geometry in Class 3?" she raised an eyebrow.

Utsav didn't answer. He was melting. He had spotted Aditi looking out the window, her hair falling like a dark curtain. He stood there smiling like an idiot at a girl who wasn't even looking at him.

"Boy!" Mrs. Suman slammed a ruler on the desk.

Utsav jumped, stammered, "Actually, blue will do!" and ran out empty-handed as 3-B roared with laughter.

The Water Cooler Marathon

Utsav decided the best way to see Aditi was walking past her door repeatedly under the guise of filling his water bottle. On his fifth trip, walking in slow motion to peer through the crack, he walked straight into Sailesh, the "Don" of 3-B.

Splurt.

In pure panic, Utsav sprayed a mouthful of water all over Sailesh's shirt.

Sailesh lifted Utsav by the shoulders. "Oye, Topper! Are you a fountain?"

Terrified, Utsav looked past Sailesh and saw Aditi blinking in confusion at the dripping wet boy. Utsav spilled the remaining water from his mouth, wriggled out like a slippery eel, and ran back to 3-A.

The "Wrong Notebook" Ruse

Utsav found a random notebook in the corridor and marched to 3-B, announcing to Mr. Abhishek that he had found "someone's property," hoping to go desk to desk.

Mr. Abhishek took it and sighed. "Utsav. This is your notebook."

The class went silent. Aditi looked up. Utsav froze. It was his own Hindi homework.

"You came all the way from Section A to return your own notebook to Section B?"

The class erupted. Utsav's face burned tomato-red. He risked one look at Aditi. She wasn't laughing; she just looked mildly puzzled. Defeated and humiliated, he grabbed his notebook and walked back. But he was secretly happy. For three seconds, she had looked at him. That was worth the shame.

A single glimpse fueled Utsav for twenty-four hours. The Morning Assembly was his daily temple. While others closed their eyes to pray, Utsav craned his neck to spot 3-B.

Aditi made the entire school stop. Male teachers spoke in soft tones; boys from Class 1 to 5 were secretly in love with her; and girls burned with jealousy over her flawless uniform, clear skin, and impossible hair. Utsav was her most shameless fan. He didn't care who saw him staring.

But talking to her was a disaster. To Aditi, Utsav was just a random boy who appeared at odd times, said odd things, and self-destructed.

The "Stone" Eraser Incident

Convinced Aditi had dropped something, Utsav sprinted to her during tiffin time.

"Excuse me, Aditi? I think you dropped your eraser."

Aditi chewed slowly, looking confused. "But Utsav... that is a white stone."

Panicking, he said, "Oh. Right. I... I collect rocks! Bye!" He threw the gravel over his shoulder and bolted.

The "Good Morning" Glitch

At 2:00 PM, school ended. Utsav rehearsed a cool goodbye. He walked up, his heart hammering.

"Good Morning, Aditi!"

Aditi stopped, looking at the setting sun. "Utsav... school is over. We are going home."

Brain freezing, Utsav blurted, "Yes. But... it is morning in America?"

Aditi gave him a puzzled look, nodded politely, and walked away.

He was a *namuna* of the highest order, but he was *her namuna*. She just didn't know it yet.

To Utsav, love was a contract. Though Aditi didn't know he existed, he considered himself "taken." He treated other girls in 3-A like they were radioactive, believing his eyes, time, and heart were reserved solely for Aditi.

But while his heart belonged to Aditi, his brain was at war with Anshu.

The rivalry was personal. Utsav had been the undisputed King of Class 1. He skipped Class 2 to stay with a friend, landing in a shark tank. When he saw Anshu's perfect test papers, he realized natural intelligence wasn't enough. He had to bleed ink to beat her.

As Half-Yearly exams approached, Utsav turned into a monk. While others traded Pokémon cards, Utsav paced furiously on his roof every evening, reciting definitions loudly until he had memorized every comma. Once, during a power cut, he passed out mid-sentence on the floor, cheek pressed against his notebook, trying to absorb knowledge by osmosis.

Results day arrived. The air was heavy.

"Second Rank," the teacher announced, "Utsav. With 574 marks out of 600."

574 was brilliant. But then came the hammer blow.

"First Rank, as always, Anshu. With 588 marks."

The 14-mark gap felt like 14 miles. Anshu soaked in the applause, looking bored. Crushed, Utsav realized all his pacing wasn't enough.

Then came news from Section B. "The topper is the new girl, Aditi. She scored 560."

Utsav's head snapped up. If he had been in Section B with his 574, he would be the King, and Aditi the Queen. They would be the Topper Duo. Instead, he was stuck in Section A, watching Anshu look down at everyone.

He hated that look. He hated that Anshu stood between him and the glory he wanted to present to Aditi. Wiping away his disappointment, he made a silent vow to Anshu: *Enjoy the applause today. In the Finals, the only hands clapping will be for me.*

When a boy's heart breaks even slightly, a terrifying alchemy occurs. Utsav's romantic fervor was funneled entirely into monomaniacal academic supremacy. He stopped looking out the window at 3-B. Gazing was passive. To be truly seen, he had to become undeniable. The boy who was "just a namuna" had to die so the "Topper" could rise.

Utsav withdrew into asceticism. The library became his sanctuary. He visualized his name above Anshu's on the notice board. His transformation was absolute.

The Pre-emptive Strike

Mr. Gupta often posed "High Order Thinking Skills" questions in Math. Usually, Anshu's hand shot up first. But one Thursday, before Mr. Gupta finished chalking a complex fractional equation, Utsav stood up.

"The remainder is 5/8, Sir," his voice cut through the silence.

Anshu's hand froze. Mr. Gupta turned, bewildered. "I haven't even finished the question."

"You didn't need to," Utsav replied with feverish intensity. "I extrapolated the sequence. The variable leads inevitably to 5/8."

For the first time, Anshu shifted uncomfortably. The predator had become the prey.

The Cartographic Masterpiece

Mrs. Rao, exacting in her standards, displayed Utsav's "Plant Anatomy" homework to the class.

"This," she announced, "is not homework. This is art."

While Anshu's work was clinically precise, Utsav's was rendered. Every root hair was detailed, xylem and phloem color-coded obsessively. He hadn't just studied it; he had devoured it.

The Inquisition

Utsav turned Social Studies into an interrogation room. While others memorized the planets, Utsav raised his hand.

"Sir, if Jupiter is a gas giant, how do we define its surface? And if Earth's rotation is constant, why is the atmospheric drag not palpable?"

The teacher paused, forced to access university-level knowledge. "That... is a concept for the ninth grade, Utsav."

Utsav simply nodded and wrote it down. He wasn't showing off; he was expanding the battlefield. He was preparing for a war where second place was no longer an option. Aditi was still the destination, but for now, books were the only road he was willing to walk.

January 26, 2011.
Republic Day.

The crisp winter morning turned breath into fog, but Utsav was burning with the heat of perfectionism.

He wasn't new to the stage. In 2010, as a five-year-old in Class 1, he had played Lord Krishna during Republic Day. The magic of that performance was crafted by Aadil Bhaiya.

"Put your thumbs in both your ears, wiggle your remaining four fingers in the air, and stick your tongue out to tease the Gopis," Aadil had instructed with his trademark infectious smile.

Utsav executed that exact pose so convincingly that he earned a 500-rupee cash prize from the Chief Guest—a fortune back then. He had also recited a profound, self-written poem about nature.

That was Utsav: precocious and deep. But now, in 2011, the stakes were higher. Even after officially leaving the school, the charismatic senior from Ether Enclave frequently returned to Vidya International to teach acting. It was Aadil Bhaiya who had knelt on the dusty stage during rehearsals, showing tiny Utsav the exact way to bring the deity to life.

He was defying biology and academia, having physically aged one year but leaping two grades academically.

"You are taking a headache upon yourself, Madam," the principal had warned his mother about the jump from Class 1 to Class 3. "The syllabus gap is huge. He will struggle to even pass."

Utsav, his feet dangling off the chair, had leaned forward. "I will definitely do it, Sir. I will be the best."

He meant it. He wanted to be the perfect student, actor, and poet. Mostly, he wanted to be perfect for Aditi.

She was backstage too, performing a dance. Utsav wanted to command her attention by being magnificent.

He had two roles. First, a poor farmer in a play about corruption. Aadil Bhaiya had been there during the January rehearsals, teaching the boys how to project raw emotion to the back rows. In the climax, a politician's son shoots him. Utsav didn't just fall; channeling Aadil's dramatic lessons, he threw himself onto the hard wooden stage with violent realism. His shoulder slammed the floorboards, shooting sharp pain up his arm, but he didn't flinch. He lay dead, holding his breath until the curtain dropped.

Backstage, rubbing his throbbing shoulder, he had no time for pain. He wiped off the farmer dust, adjusted his white kurta, and grabbed the microphone to recite his poem about the martyr Bhagat Singh.

He was reciting for the ghosts of freedom fighters, but performing for the girl in the wings.

His passionate voice echoed through the chilly grounds. Delivering the last line, he looked toward the side of the stage.

There was Aditi, dressed in her shimmering costume. And for the first time, she was looking straight at him.

Not past him. Not confused. Her eyes were fixed on him, attentive and silent.

Utsav's heart hammered. Time froze. A pure surge of triumph made him dizzy. *She sees me,* he thought.

He didn't realize she was only watching him intently because she was next in the lineup, waiting for him to finish so she could dance. But facts didn't matter. Walking off stage, nursing his bruised shoulder, Utsav felt he had won the Nobel Prize. For ten seconds, it was just the Poet and his Muse.

February melted into March. The school air smelled of panic and printer ink. Final Exams were approaching.

For Utsav, this was a reckoning. He turned his brain into a fortress, etching every definition and formula into his grey matter. While others ran around begging for important questions, Utsav sat still.

The only other island of calm in that ocean of panic was Anshu.

But their silence was different. Utsav's was a bomb waiting to explode. Anshu's was a mountain—unmoved and ancient.

Utsav remembered clapping for Anshu on Prize Day when she was in Class 2, unaware she would become his arch-nemesis. Now, he watched her like a hawk, fighting a war for the throne. Anshu? She was just living her life, knowing the throne had her name on it since LKG.

In those final weeks, Utsav fought a battle to the death, while Anshu didn't even know there was a war.

The "IMP" Question Standoff

In the last Science class, students swarmed Mrs. Rao's desk for important questions. Utsav remained rigidly in his seat. He knew the entire book. He looked at Anshu, who was also sitting, detached from the mob.

See? She knows I'm watching, Utsav thought, mentally arm-wrestling her. *It's a test of nerves.*

Meanwhile, oblivious Anshu was just trying to peel a sticker off her new pencil box without tearing it. She didn't turn around.

The Blackboard Duel

Mr. Gupta called Utsav and Anshu to the board to solve a complex division problem. Utsav sprang up, his hand moving in a blur of math. He wanted to finish first and look at her with victory in his eyes. He finished in record time, drew a double line, and turned, chest heaving.

Anshu was still writing calmly, her numbers perfectly aligned. Finishing ten seconds later, she dusted her fingers and walked back without glancing at Utsav's board. Deflated, Utsav realized she treated him like furniture.

The Library Cold War

During self-study in the library, Utsav sat opposite Anshu for a psychological showdown. He opened his Social Studies book; she opened English.

Utsav decided to match her pace, turning his page only when she did to prove his processing speed.

Snap. Anshu turned a page.

Utsav instantly turned his. Snap. Another page.

Sweating and hyperventilating, Utsav read faster than ever, thinking, *I am keeping up with the Queen.*

After ten minutes, Anshu sighed, closed her book, and pulled out a comic.

Utsav froze. *Is she giving up?* Then he realized the truth. She hadn't been studying; she was just skimming page numbers because she was bored. While he was racing, she was taking a break.

The exams arrived with a nervous quiet. Every student was locked in a private battle with the syllabus.

But Utsav's defining moment happened outside the door, five minutes before the first paper.

He was mentally revising formulas when a soft voice interrupted. "All the best, Utsav."

He froze and turned. It was Aditi.

For the first time, the Muse had spoken to the Poet. A normal person would have said, "Thank you, same to you."

But Utsav’s brain short-circuited. Panicked, he blurted the first true fact that came to mind: "You have such long hair."

Silence.

Aditi blinked in genuine confusion, touching her hair self-consciously.

Realizing he sounded like a lunatic, Utsav’s survival instincts kicked in. "I mean... All the very best to you too! I know you will top the finals. You are... very smart."

Aditi gave a polite, bewildered smile and walked into her exam hall. Utsav stood there, banging his forehead against the wall.

The exams ended, leaving a vacuum of silence and a ten-day purgatory before results.

Utsav was physically broken. He had pressed his pen so hard in his quest for perfection that his fingertips throbbed four days later—a soldier's wounds from a war fought with ink.

To escape the anxiety, Utsav retreated to his grandfather's house. Dadaji was a literary giant, a poet living among dusty books, and the only person who understood the storm inside Utsav's head. While others played cricket, Utsav sat in the library reading spiritual texts and philosophy, trying to calm his restless heart.

But excitement bubbled in his chest. He knew a golden school rule: the Top 5 students from every section were promoted to the "Superior Section" of the next class. The Top 5 from Class 3-B would move to Class 4-A.

Utsav did the math. Aditi had topped 3-B in the half-yearlys. There was zero doubt she would top the finals.

The realization made his heart race. She was coming to Section A.

There would be no running to the water cooler or inventing excuses to borrow a duster. She would sit in the same room, breathing the same air.

Nursing his sore fingers in the library, Utsav smiled. He didn't care if Anshu topped or if he topped. The walls between Section A and Section B were about to crumble. His muse, his "long-haired" distraction, was finally coming home.

March 31, 2011.
The day of judgment.

Utsav walked into school without a bag, but carrying something heavier: Hope. He was prepared to collect his result card, his promotion letter, and the confirmation of his victory.

The assembly buzzed. Utsav vibrated with nervous energy, willing Mr. Gupta to end the suspense of the Principal's speech. Finally, Mr. Gupta stepped forward with the list.

He began with the juniors. Utsav's palms sweat. Then came Class 3-B.

"The First Rank for Class 3-B goes to Aditi, with 532 marks."

Utsav exhaled. He knew it. Aditi had conquered her section. The Muse was coming to Section A.

Now, his turn. The battlefield of 3-A.

"Third Rank... Namrata."

Clapping ensued. Utsav straightened. In his head, the script was written: Anshu for Second Rank, and him as Topper.

"The Second Rank," Mr. Gupta said.

Utsav instinctively turned to Anshu, expecting her to stand. But Anshu sat statuesque and calm. Utsav frowned.

Suddenly, a sharp pain shot through his arm. Akhil and Shyam pinched him hard.

"Oye! Go!" Shyam whispered urgently.

"What?" Utsav looked confused.

"It's you, idiot!" Akhil hissed. "He called your name!"

The world tilted. The class was looking at him. Mr. Gupta was looking at him.

Second Rank... Utsav. No. That couldn't be right. He had studied until his fingers bled. He stumbled forward, mind racing. There had to be a calculation error. He rushed to grab the result sheet. "Sir, wait—"

Mr. Gupta gently stopped him, handing him the card. "Congratulations, Utsav."

"And the First Rank goes to Anshu, with 579 marks."

Utsav looked down. *577.* 579 versus 577. The gap was barely a breath. A spelling mistake. But it was enough.

He stood holding the paper declaring him the "Silver Boy" again. The tragedy was the poetry of the number. He came in Rank 2. Because of 2 marks.

He looked at Anshu walking to claim the throne. He only heard the mocking echo of those missing marks. His perfection had fallen exactly two steps short.

The applause sounded like static. But amidst the sea of clapping, one pair clapped with genuine sincerity. Aditi. She had seen him clap for her. But she frowned. He didn't look like a second-ranker; he looked like a defeated general.

She leaned toward Preeti. "Why is he so quiet? He came second. That is good, isn't it?"

Preeti, knowing playground gossip better than multiplication tables, leaned in. "He isn't just a second ranker. Utsav was a Topper. But he decided to skip Class 2 entirely. They both crashed into Class 3. Because he skipped Class 2, he got exactly 2 marks less."

It was mythic playground logic, but it made perfect sense to them. The skipped year had exacted a tax of two marks.

After assembly, parents swarmed the teachers. Aditi found an opening and walked up to Utsav. He was staring at the gap between 577 and 579.

"Congratulations on coming second," she said softly.

Utsav looked up, startled.

"Don't worry," she added with innocent optimism. "You will top Class 4."

She didn't know she was walking into the lion's den. He decided to unfold the map of their future.

"It’s not that simple, Aditi," his voice was serious. "Do you know the rule of Vidya International School?"

She shook her head.

"They crash the toppers together. They take the best from every section and put them in one room to make the competition great." He stepped closer. "Next year, you won't just be watching. You will see both of us—Anshu and me—as your competitors. Or maybe," he paused, a challenging smile touching his lips, "you will perform so well that I will become the one who is jealous."

He left the words hanging like a prophecy. Aditi stood blinking. She came to offer sympathy and was handed a declaration of war. She watched him walk away, utterly confused by a boy who congratulated you by threatening jealousy.

Aditi's mind swirled. At nine, three years older than Utsav, she should have been wiser. Yet, standing before that six-year-old speaking of "crashing toppers," she felt immature. She went to her dad, her victory feeling different. She had met her match.

Utsav walked home, head hung low. The house was full of love, but devoid of peace. His family hovered, offering sweets and praise. It bounced off him. His grief was born from an unchosen struggle, honoring a friendship, and a perfectionism eating him alive.

The family deployed their "One Shot Solution": calling Bhaiya.

Utsav's bond with his brother was unbeatable. Bhaiya was his soul's compass. Mom explained the "Case of the 2 Marks Gap" and handed Utsav the phone.

"Hello?" Utsav squeaked.

"So, I heard you decided to leave two marks for charity?" Bhaiya's warm voice crackled.

A tear rolled down Utsav's cheek. "I lost, Bhaiya. I worked so hard. But Anshu got 579 and I got 577. I am second again."

Bhaiya paused, turning serious. "Utsav, do you know why there is a gap of two marks? Because you bought time. Anshu spent one year in Class 1 and one in Class 2. You paid those two marks as a fee to skip an entire year. You are six years old, fighting with eight and nine-year-olds, and almost beat them."

Utsav wiped his eyes.

"But Bhaiya, second is still second. The world remembers the winner."

"The world remembers the story, babu. Anshu won a rank. You won a year. That '2' isn't a failure. It's space God left so you have a reason to run faster in Class 4. You love the chase more than the trophy. Are you going to cry over two marks, or prepare for the girl coming to your class?"

"How do you know about her?"

Bhaiya laughed. "I know everything. Go wash your face. We don't cry over silver; we polish it until it blinds them."

Utsav hung up. The grief wasn't gone; it was fuel. The war wasn't over. It had just begun.

The phone call was an ointment. Utsav breathed easily. The family went out for dinner to celebrate the effort.

As he ate, a new equation formed. He had lost the title, but gained Aditi. She would be promoted to Section A. He would see her every day.

Then, realization hit him like cold water. The hurdle of admission.

Admission to Section A was about speed. The "Superior Section" filled quickly. You had to submit fees within 5 days. It was reserved for geniuses and the wealthy. Anshu and Aditi belonged to the latter. Their seats were likely locked. Utsav hadn't secured his yet.

After dinner, Utsav looked at his mother. "Mummy. We need to submit the fees for Class 4. Section A fills up fast."

His mother looked concerned. "Section A has cut-throat competition. Are you sure? Section B might be less stressful."

Utsav shook his head. He couldn't say the competition had long hair and innocent eyes. He argued with ambition. "I can handle it. I know it is tough. But I will outperform them. Just get me into Section A."

He argued with ferocity, desperate to ensure the gap between him and Aditi didn't become a wall.

Love won. On April 1st, his mother submitted the fees. Utsav was officially in Class 4, Section A.

The receipt was a visa to paradise. But the real prize was on the counter. While his mother signed forms, Utsav peeked at the "Fee Register." Under "Paid" for Class 4-A: *Aditi.*

Utsav let out a held breath. Seeing her name was a soothing balm. The trophy was lost, but the prize secured.

Now began the "Wait of the Seven Days" for Roll Numbers. A school rumor dictated: "If a boy and a girl have subsequent roll numbers, they are destined to end up dating."

Utsav took this seriously. He spent the week praying for a number next to hers.

April 7th. The list was pinned. He traced the "A"s.

Roll No. 5: Aditi. He looked down one line.

Roll No. 6: Preeti. His stomach dropped.

Roll No. 7: Utsav. A gap named Preeti. The prophecy shattered. Frustration washed over him. He couldn't tolerate the distance again. After fighting wars and skipping grades to be near her, Fate placed a human barrier between them.

To understand his frustration, you must understand the geography. Section A wasn't just a classroom; it was Olympus on the Top Floor. It smelled of floor cleaner, not chalk dust. It had dedicated security and private restrooms. It was a gated community.

For Aditi, stepping into this room was a victory. She wanted the sophistication of Section A. She walked in light and relieved, unaware of Utsav's gaze.

But to Utsav, Section A was the stage for The Unnamed Relationship. He was fiercely protective of their invisible bond. Preeti—Roll Number 6—felt like a physical wound. He sat staring at Preeti's head, seething at the intrusion. While Aditi sat glowing in the front row, Utsav sulked two seats behind, angry he had to share paradise with a third wheel.

For forty days, Utsav lived in delirious happiness. The seating arrangement—girls on the left, boys on the right—was his best friend. Sitting on the right, he could stare in Aditi's direction. Whenever she turned, he expertly shifted his focus past her ear out the window.

I am not looking at you. I am looking at nature, his eyes lied.

Aditi glowed with an unearthly beauty. She was a vision of innocence, and Utsav was her secret worshipper.

But happiness has an expiration date. May 20th. "Summer Vacation starts tomorrow. School reopens on June 20th."

While others cheered, Utsav felt sentenced to solitary confinement. Thirty days. 720 hours. No glimpses.

He tried to be a normal 7-year-old, but nothing works when your heart is stuck in 4-A.

The "Dead" Batsman

Playing neighborhood cricket, Utsav received an easy full toss. But he was distracted, looking at a passing white car. *Is that her car? Clack.* The ball hit the stumps. "Too hot," he muttered, handing the bat back. It wasn't the sun; it was the coldness of her absence.

The Calendar Surgery

Desperate, Utsav violently scribbled out dates on the calendar with a red marker. Caught crossing out May 27th at 10 AM, he told his mother dramatically, "This day is useless," and hid under his sheets, hoping to wake up in June.

In early June, a terrifying thought hit him. He imagined school reopening. First test scores announced. Anshu standing as topper, and Aditi clapping for her.

His blood ran cold. *Aditi is the dream, but Anshu is the reality.* Love wasn't enough. If he wanted to be worthy of Aditi, he couldn't be a loser. He had to be the King. He had a duty to his parents, to Bhaiya, and a burning obstinacy to crush Anshu.

He made a strategic decision. Aditi would no longer be a distraction; she would be fuel.

"I will study so hard that the answers will appear before the questions," he vowed.

The remaining twenty days were a boot camp. Locked in his room, he dissected chapters, memorized definitions, and practiced cursive until calluses formed. The Quarterly Exams were the first battle of the new era.

He worked with terrifying silence, telling himself every hour Anshu played was an hour he gained. By June 20th, he was a loaded gun waiting for the trigger.

June brought heat, but for Utsav, sunrise.

He became the phantom of the morning, arriving before the watchman. He threw his bag in 4-A and sprinted to the main gate facing South. To the West lay Zenith, separated by a narrow river and concrete bridge.

He waited for 7:50 AM. When she appeared, the world shifted.

Aditi didn't walk; she floated. Her long, dark hair danced in the wind like a dark cloud trailing a star. Her pristine white skin flushed crimson in the sun. She was a glass doll in a stone quarry.

Utsav wanted to lay himself down so no dust touched her feet. He watched the most beautiful girl walk past, unaware he had stood there for an hour just to watch her cross a bridge. Ambition didn't exist in those ten minutes. Only the girl who walked on air.

The Quarterly Exams arrived. Utsav solved equations, but his mind was in 4-A. Education was secondary; observation was his primary subject. No words were exchanged, yet the silence was melodious.

The Gust and the Veil

A gust of wind caught Aditi's hair, blowing it across her face like a midnight veil. Utsav held his breath as she struggled to tuck it behind her ear, terrified exhaling would break the spell.

The Monsoon Reflection

During torrential rain, Aditi traced a raindrop on the window. Utsav placed his finger in the air, aligning it with her reflection. In that dimension of glass, their fingers touched, sending a jolt of electricity through him.

The Fallen Eraser

During a silent Math test, Aditi's eraser rolled into the aisle. Their eyes met. He wanted to dive for it, but the teacher barked, "Eyes on your paper!" Utsav snapped back. Aditi offered a small, apologetic smile before retrieving it. That secret connection meant more than the test.

Judgment day arrived. Mrs. Rao entered 4-A with the ledger. Utsav sat radiating confidence, ready to impress Aditi with his Second Rank.

"The First Rank goes to... Anshu. With 666."

Utsav rolled his eyes. *Now, it's my turn.* "The Second Rank... goes to Aditi. With 650."

The ground dissolved. Aditi was second? She challenged Anshu? Where was he? He stared blankly as Aditi whispered a 'Thank You.'

"And the Third Rank... goes to Utsav. With 636."

He was third. Lost to Aditi by 14 marks.

Utsav stood slowly. The applause mocked him. His world flipped. He had fantasy-built himself as her intellectual superior—her

"Hero." Reality slapped him. She was "Beauty with Brains." He had lost to the girl he wanted to impress.

Burning shame washed over him. How could he face her? Losing to Anshu was habit, but losing to Aditi assaulted his ego. He had been reduced to her "Minister."

He sank back, unable to see her beauty, crushed by his own defeat.

The Quarterlies brought a revelation. Aditi hadn't entered Section A to escape bullies. Her target was Anshu. She wanted the crown. And Anshu was an unbreachable fortress.

Utsav felt a physical tightness in his chest. While he admired the Apsara, the Apsara was sharpening her sword for war. He felt foolish. A spectator.

A terrifying seriousness descended. The boy who waited at the gate retreated into textbooks. The distance grew in silence.

The lover faded; the competitor rose.

The Unwatched Window

It was a free period, usually Utsav's "Golden Hour" to watch Aditi gaze out the window. Aditi, accustomed to his attention, turned slightly, expecting his stare.

But Utsav wasn't looking. His head was bent low, hand moving furiously over his math notebook. Aditi lingered, waiting for a secret glance. He didn't look up. The window was open, the view perfect, but Utsav had closed the blinds of his heart. She turned back, feeling a strange new chill.

The Borrowed Sharpener

During a history lecture, Utsav's pencil broke. Previously, this would be a theatrical event—an excuse to ask Aditi for a sharpener, to touch her hand. Aditi heard the snap and instinctively offered her sharpener across the aisle.

Utsav looked at it, then at her. His eyes were gentle, his smile absent. "It's okay," he whispered politely. "I have a spare."

He pulled out a second pencil and resumed writing. Aditi slowly lowered her hand. The rejection wasn't rude—it was efficient. That hurt more.

Twenty cold, studious days passed. The pressure cooker of Section A whistled with surprise tests. Then, the silence broke.

Sitting across the narrow aisle from Utsav, Aditi whispered, "Utsav."

He turned. She looked at him with curiosity and respect. "How did you know? How did you predict I would end up in this competitive position? Looking at everyone as a rival?"

A faint, nostalgic smile touched his face. "Because I have been you. In Class 1, I topped. I used to clap hardest for Anshu. I didn't know envy. But look at me now. The applause has died, and only hunger remains."

Aditi sighed. "I don't know why. From the outside, Section A looked so relaxing. But distant drums sound sweet. It is cut-throat. Everyone has this desperate need to be ahead. In my previous school, sections were just alphabets. But here..."

Utsav felt a surge of pride. "It is a Matrix," he said, sounding older than his seven years. "Designed by the Head Sir. He doesn't want anyone in a comfort zone. He knows a human must be stubborn on his field of duty. We work so hard here we could defeat the toppers of any other school."

Aditi processed his philosophy. The look in her eyes changed. She was no longer looking at a child; she was looking at an equal.

That brief, heavy conversation lingered in Utsav's mind like a fever. *She asked me. She understood.* He replayed it for four days, drifting, staring at the aisle where her voice had floated.

But the Matrix snapped him back.

He looked at Anshu's back and realized he was slipping. He was analyzing a conversation instead of the syllabus. The guilt of a soldier dropping his shield hit him.

No, Utsav told himself. *Not again.* Stubbornness took over. Love was a luxury he couldn't afford if he wanted the crown.

He dove back into his books with terrifying intensity. It became an obsession. He studied while others played, recited answers walking home, solved mental math at dinner. He became a ghost at home and a machine at school. The teachers noticed his burning purpose. The love for Aditi hadn't died, but he buried it under textbooks, promising to retrieve it only after conquering the peak.

From July to November, Utsav ceased to be a boy. He became a monk. He severed all distractions. The window was ignored. The "bridge watching" shortened. His focus was absolute. He wanted to dismantle the hierarchy and reclaim his throne from Anshu.

The Era of "By-Heart" Perfection

In 2011, "Concept" was a luxury; "Memory" was currency. Teachers wanted the textbook's answer exactly. In Section A, missing a "keyword" meant brutal deductions. That's why there were different rankers in different sections; the logistics varied. No matter your intelligence in Section B, you became average in Section A.

Aditi was different; her sole purpose had been to escape Section B after realizing the school's matrix.

Utsav adapted. He didn't just learn answers; he photographed them mentally. He was a machine of retention.

November 2011: Half-Yearly Exams

During exams, Utsav's pen moved like a metronome. The thinking was done; he was just downloading data.

He politely wished Aditi "Good Luck," but the warmth was gone. Aditi had changed too. Section A's cut-throat mentality infected her. She barely acknowledged him. To her, Utsav was a defeated soldier—a permanent Rank 3. She wasn't competing with him; she was gunning for Anshu.

December 2011: Judgment Day

Biting cold outside, unbearable heat inside Class 4-A. The results were ready.

Aditi sat upright, confident she would finally dethrone Anshu. She believed Utsav was history.

Mrs. Rao walked in, looking solemn and awestruck. "The results have set a new benchmark."

She read the list. "The Third Rank goes to Aditi. With 624 marks out of 700."

Air left Aditi's lungs. Third? She had an almost 90% average. Stunned, she assumed Utsav was second and Anshu first. Disappointment washed over her.

"The Second Rank..."

The class turned to Utsav, ready to clap for the "Silver Boy."

"...goes to Anshu. With 663 marks."

Graveyard silence. Aditi's jaw dropped. The class gasped. Anshu was Second? The Queen who hadn't lost since LKG had fallen?

If Anshu was Second... who was First?

Slowly, every head turned to the aisle seat. Utsav sat perfectly still, his face a mask of calm. He looked like a man who had already read the script.

"And the First Rank," the teacher's voice trembled, "goes to the Topper of the Class, with a historic score... Utsav. With 693 marks out of 700."

He lost only 7 marks total. One mark cut per subject, only because Section A teachers had an unwritten rule: never give full marks in theory to avoid arrogance. Otherwise, he would have scored 700/700.

CHAPTER 3

Adyutsav: A Sweetest Surrender

As his name echoed, Utsav stood up. The applause was deafening. Even Anshu was clapping in shock. Aditi stared at him as if he were a stranger.

But Utsav didn't see the class. His eyes glazed over as a flashback of the last four months played in his mind.

The Festival of Darkness

It was Diwali. The neighborhood was lit, firecrackers bursting. His cousins screamed with joy on the roof. Utsav was in his room, curtains drawn, cotton balls in his ears. He cried silently, wanting to play, but wiped the tears and continued solving his 50th Math sum. He chose the darkness of his room over the lights of the festival.

The Fever Dream

September. He was burning with a 102-degree fever. "Leave the homework," his mother pleaded. But shivering under a blanket, Utsav held his Science book. "If I sleep now, I will forget," he whispered, studying through the fever, hallucinating equations.

The Empty Window

An October evening. He heard Aditi laughing outside. Every cell screamed to run to the balcony for one glimpse. He stood up, walked to the door... and locked it. Closing the blinds, he turned his back on the girl he loved, opened his History book, and chose the past over his present.

The flashback ended. Utsav blinked, back in Class 4-A.

He looked at the teacher, then Anshu, and finally Aditi, whose eyes were wide with fear and admiration.

He didn't smile or cheer. He walked to the front, took his report card, and nodded—the bored nonchalance of a king claiming his birthright. He had sacrificed his childhood for this paper; he felt only the quiet satisfaction of a promise kept.

Inside, a thousand fireworks exploded. He wanted to scream, "I did it! I beat the Queen!" But outside, he was ice. He tapped his pen as if his historic 693/700 was just another Tuesday. He wanted them to think, *Of course Utsav topped. That was the plan.*

He accepted handshakes with a stiff nod and Anshu's stunned look with a casual shrug. He played the "Born Genius" perfectly.

But the acting stopped the moment his eyes crossed the aisle.

The fireworks died. The celebration turned to cold water.

Aditi sat staring at her report card. She wasn't crying, but her face looked like a cracked porcelain vase.

Her strategy had been simple: Beat Anshu. She had burned herself in the fire of hard work, sacrificing everything to cross Anshu. But the dice rolled an unexpected number. She hadn't just failed to beat Anshu (now Rank 2); she had been pushed down to Rank 3 by a ghost rising from the ashes.

She didn't have one mountain to climb; she had two.

Utsav knew her parents considered "Second" the first loser. The weight of expectations crushed her shoulders. Her radiant, fairy-like charm was gone, replaced by the gray shadow of failure.

Utsav stared. The obsession with marks evaporated. He looked at his Rank 1 report card, then at her sadness.

The math didn't add up. Winning was supposed to make him a King. But seeing the girl who made his life beautiful look so defeated made him feel like a villain.

I did this, he realized with a jolt of guilt. *My victory is the reason for her pain.* In his mad rush to satisfy his ego, he had trampled the heart of the one person he truly cared about. What was the point of applause if Aditi wasn't clapping?

A profound wisdom settled over him. In the game of love, classroom rules don't apply. *Sometimes,* Utsav thought, *winning everything isn't the goal. Sometimes, you have to lose to make someone else shine.* The fierce academic warrior died; the Lover was reborn. He didn't want this crown if it meant Aditi had to cry. He had proven his point. He could top if he wanted to. But from now on, he wouldn't mind stepping back. A King can survive without a throne, but a Poet cannot survive without his Muse's smile.

The Architecture of Sacrifice

Guilt transformed Utsav. The boy who memorized textbooks now devised a plan to lose marks.

In the 2012 Final Examinations, he would intentionally mark himself to come in second. It wasn't laziness; it was calculated martyrdom.

Utsav was possessive, protective, and obsessive—traits absorbed from his idol, his Bhaiya. He loved Aditi with pride. He wanted her to top, to stand on stage while the entire school realized how breathtaking she was. In a twisted way, he wanted to show the world, *Look at her. She is the best. And she is my choice.*

The "By-Heart" genius decided to become the "Calculated Loser." He would hand her the crown because he couldn't bear the risk of her losing again.

The Illusion of Arrogance

As Final Exams approached, Aditi turned into a hermit, working with terrifying dedication to prove Rank 3 was a glitch.

Utsav, however, was eerily calm. The class whispered his fire had burned out. Even teachers misinterpreted his silence. "Overconfidence," Mrs. Rao whispered. "He topped once, and now he thinks he is untouchable. The arrogance of success has gotten to his head."

They saw arrogance, not sacrifice. They didn't know Utsav was mentally rehearsing which answers to delete and definitions to shorten. He was studying how to fail just enough to let his Muse win.

On the day of the first exam, Utsav scanned the crowd and found Aditi near the old Neem tree, muttering formulas.

Hesitating, he picked up a smooth, ordinary grey pebble and walked over.

"Hey," he whispered.

"Hello, Utsav."

"Aditi, I... I don't know how to say this. I was so obsessed with defeating Anshu that I didn't realize I dragged you into the competition too. I never wanted to be your rival."

"Do you know, Utsav," Aditi interrupted, looking at the tree. "Last year, you told me, 'Next year, you won't just be watching. You will see Anshu and me as competitors. Or maybe you will perform so well I will become jealous.'"

Utsav froze. She remembered.

"I didn't understand then," she turned to him. "But now I realize how much this competition affects a person. Last year I clapped for you. Today, I look at you as a rival. It’s strange."

Utsav’s heart ached. "Aditi," he said firmly. "You are the best. We are not competitors. There should be only one goal: No one should come First except you."

He laughed a hollow laugh. "My First Rank was just luck. My real luck..." He held out the ordinary stone. "...is in this stone."

Aditi looked at the pebble.

"I keep it as my lucky charm," Utsav lied with conviction. "Keep it in your pocket. You are the best, and this stone will bring you the First Rank."

Aditi hesitantly took it, and a genuine smile finally broke through her stress. She didn't know it was just gravel, and that the real luck was the boy standing before her, about to mark answers wrong just to keep her smiling.

Call it the "Placebo Effect," but that grey stone changed everything.

Aditi transformed into a warrior. During every exam, she placed the ordinary stone on her desk like a holy talisman. When stuck, she touched it, remembered Utsav's confidence, and wrote with unprecedented ferocity.

Meanwhile, Utsav curated the scoreboard. In Math, he skipped a step. In Science, he labeled a diagram wrong. He bled marks on purpose, calculating to land safely at Rank 2 and push Aditi to Rank 1. A dangerous gamble blinded by love.

The Calculation Error

Result Day arrived.

"The First Rank," the teacher beamed, "goes to Aditi. With a magnificent score of 677/700."

The class erupted. Glowing, Aditi looked at the stone and smiled.

Utsav clapped the hardest. *Plan successful. Now, I will be Second.*

"The Second Rank goes to Anshu. With 670/700."

Utsav's clap froze. If Anshu was 670...

"And the Third Rank goes to Utsav. With 664/700."

He had overdone it. He cut too deep, underestimating Anshu's consistency and overestimating his "controlled failure." He had stumbled down two steps.

For a genius, falling to Rank 3 was a tactical disaster. But Utsav didn't look humiliated. He looked triumphant.

Because he was looking at the room. The boys stared in awe; the girls with admiration. Aditi looked breathtaking, her cheeks flushed, eyes sparkling like a queen claiming her kingdom.

Look at her, his heart swelled. *She is winning because I stepped back.* He didn't care about 664. He had successfully showcased his "Choice" to the world.

When the applause died, Aditi turned and locked eyes with Utsav. She smiled a dazzling smile meant only for him and held up the stone. In that smile, Utsav found his First Rank. Her happiness was the real result. He had lost the academic battle, but he knew he had won the war.

The Hangover of Heroism

Utsav floated home, feeling like a tragic Bollywood hero. But he forgot one crucial variable: Home.

The moment he stepped inside, the cloud evaporated. In the living room, the report card was just a document of decline.

He handed it to his mother. "Result?" she asked.

She scanned the columns. Her eyebrows knit. "Third?" The word hung like an accusation.

"In the Half-Yearly, you were First with 693. Now Third with 664. What happened?"

Utsav stood with his head bowed. He couldn't say, *I marked questions wrong so a girl would smile.* "You lost marks in the diagram labeling?" she pointed. "You drew this perfectly in your rough notebook last week! And Math? A calculation error? You solve these in your sleep."

To the teacher, it was a mistake. To his mother, it was carelessness.

Her eyes turned watery. "We put you in Section A to learn from the best. Papa works hard to pay fees. And you go backwards? Are you tired of studying? Has success gone to your head?"

The "romantic sacrifice" suddenly felt stupid. In his quest to make Aditi happy, he made his mother cry. Euphoria was replaced by crushing guilt.

"Go to your room," she said.

Utsav realized being a hero comes with a price, paid by those who love you most.

The Investigation

At dinner, the atmosphere was heavy. Utsav ate silently. Later, his parents whispered.

"He knows the answers, Suresh," his mother said. "How can he forget them?"

"Go to the school tomorrow. Talk to the Principal," his father suggested.

The next morning, Utsav's mother marched into the Principal's office. "I need to understand this fluctuation. Why did he drop almost 30 marks?"

"Utsav is a special case," the Principal sighed. "He skipped Class 2. Maybe the foundation is missing, and he is struggling to cope."

"No, Sir. If it was the foundation, he wouldn't have topped the Half-Yearly. He practices for hours. This isn't lack of capability; it is lack of execution."

The Principal tapped his pen. "He is brilliant, Ma'am. But Anshu and Aditi don't just rely on school teaching. They go to professional coaching. They practice sample papers two grades above their level. That is their 'edge.' Utsav is fighting with a sword. They are fighting with cannons. It's a matter of resources."

The Principal implied it was a "pay-to-win" game. Utsav was Third because he lacked the privilege of extra tuition.

Mother stared at the "Rank 3". Her hesitation vanished, replaced by fierce resolve.

"If a gap of privilege is the only thing standing between my child and his future, then that gap ends today," she stated firmly. "I will cut down on my needs, but I will not let a lack of resources be the wall that stops him. Where do I send him?"

The Principal nodded with newfound respect. "This is Gupta Sir."

A giant, 6-foot-tall man with broad shoulders stood up from the corner. "The boy has fire, Madam," his deep voice resonated. "Send him to me. I will not just teach him subjects; I will teach him discipline."

The self-study era was over. Professional training had begun.

Class 5 began with military-grade clockwork. No playful afternoons. At 4:00 PM, he reported to Gupta Sir’s Coaching Centre.

Gupta Sir was a sculptor. On the first day, Utsav quickly scribbled answers. *10+20x2 = 50.* Gupta Sir circled the 50 in red ink. "Look at your zero. Why is it half the size of the five? In Mathematics, symmetry is everything. A small zero looks like a mistake. Toppers don't just get the right answer; they present it with respect."

He drew a perfect 50. The digits were identical in height. "From today, your Zero will be as big as your numbers."

Utsav spent two days writing perfectly symmetrical numbers. He realized perfection wasn't just what you know, but how you show it.

Utsav walked to coaching every day because the system demanded it. The fire of the "Topper" burned, but he chose to cap the volcano. He wanted to be the "Guardian"—Aditi at Rank 1, him at Rank 2. As long as she was smiling at the top, he was content.

At the coaching center, Utsav was a misfit placed with students three years older. He hated Class 5 Algebra but mastered English grammar easily, thanks to Dadaji. He sat bored, mentally correcting the seniors' tenses—a Ferrari stuck in traffic.

As the youngest, the senior girls found him adorable, trying to pinch his cheeks and play. But Utsav was stone. He pulled away unsmiling. If Aditi wasn't touching him, he didn't want anyone to. He was a one-woman man in a seven-year-old's body.

When June arrived, Utsav ran to Class 5-A, desperate for a glimpse of Aditi.

But "Heaven" had been breached. Seven brilliant students transferred out, and seven from Section B replaced them. These were the Bullies. The disciplined air was polluted with slang, paper balls, and aggression.

For the first ten days, Utsav faced a strange new war. Small and quiet, he was a perfect target. He had the intellect to outsmart them and the rage to fight back, but he chose silence. He didn't want to disturb Aditi or ruin the decorum she loved. He endured.

The "Accidental" Trip

Rohan stretched his leg out. Utsav stumbled and fell hard on his knees. The class giggled. Utsav stood, dusted his knees, and walked to the teacher's desk, treating Rohan like a speed bump.

The Tiffin Tax

During recess, Vikram and Sameer snatched Utsav's aloo paratha. Utsav closed his tiffin calmly. "You can have it. You look like you need it more." He went hungry, refusing to give them the satisfaction.

The Ink Stain

Bullies flicked blue ink onto Utsav's pristine white shirt. "New design!" they mocked. Rage boiled in his veins. He clenched his fist, but looked at Aditi writing peacefully in the front row. He unclenched his fist, ignoring the stain like a battle scar.

By July, Utsav dodged bullies and waited for the magic. And it always happened.

No matter how angry or hungry he was, when his eyes landed on Aditi, the steam vanished. Utsav was boiling milk; Aditi was a sprinkle of cold water. One look at her, completely unaware of the chaos, and his anger cooled.

To Aditi, Utsav was just furniture. She had no idea he fought a daily war just to share her air, or that her presence kept his volcano from erupting. She was his peace. He was her invisible shadow.

July 16, 2012.

A date changed the geopolitics of Utsav's life. His mother, perpetually worried about her "sensitive" son in a school of bullies, played her trump card: she got Badi Didi a job as the Science Teacher at Vidya International.

For Utsav, this was a double-edged sword. He had immunity as the "Teacher's Brother," but was under 24/7 surveillance. Lonely walks became bicycle rides with his sister. He lived a double life—a disciplined brother near the Science Lab, and a lovesick devotee near 5-A.

Didi wasn't just a chaperone; she was a manager. Noticing Gupta Sir wasting twenty minutes of coaching on cursive drills, she marched in.

"Sir, Utsav is here to learn concepts, not calligraphy. Please utilize this hour for Math and English," she said firmly. Gupta Sir nodded, realizing Utsav's formidable support system.

Didi became Utsav's "Iron Shield." A single glare from the Science Ma'am sent bullies scurrying. But she couldn't protect his heart.

During a Monthly Test held on the playground, Utsav finished early. Walking to submit his paper, his radar pinged: Aditi. She sat under a Neem tree, looking stressed.

"How is it going?" he whispered, checking for teachers.

"I am leaving a 3-mark question blank," she sighed, defeated. "I can't remember the second point."

"It's okay. Submit whatever you have done."

He walked away, calculating. *She is losing 3 marks. If I submit my full paper, the gap will widen. She will feel bad.*

Hidden behind a bush, Utsav looked at his perfect 5-mark answer on the last page. *Rrrippp.* He tore it out, crumbled it, and threw it away. He sacrificed 5 marks to compensate for her 3.

He didn't tell her; charity would hurt her pride. He sabotaged his victory in silence, an invisible guardian protecting her happiness from himself.

With Didi patrolling, Utsav's fear evaporated. He walked with his head high, answering questions, looking bullies in the eye.

But bullies are slow learners. Surya, Gupta Sir's cousin, relied on his lineage for immunity. Sitting behind Utsav, bored Surya violently rubbed the baby hairs on Utsav's neck upward. The stinging pain made Utsav flinch, dropping his pen. His neck turned angry red.

The door swung open. Didi had arrived. She saw Utsav rubbing his neck. The room temperature dropped.

"Who did this?" she asked dangerously.

Aradhya stood up. "Surya did it."

Surya smirked. Didi walked to his desk. Looking at his naturally crooked fingers, she leaned in. "I don't care whose cousin you are. If you ever touch Utsav again... these fingers are already crooked. Next time, I will break them."

Surya's smirk vanished. The clinical threat terrified him. The bullies treated Utsav like radioactive material after that.

While Didi was a dragon to bullies, she noticed Utsav's blind spot: Aditi. Aditi remained neutral, but Utsav was transparent glass.

The Water Bottle Service

Didi saw Aditi coughing. Instantly, Utsav unscrewed his bottle and offered it with both hands like a deity's offering. Aditi drank and returned it casually. Utsav looked at the bottle like a holy relic. Didi smiled. *Oh Utsav, you are gone.*

The Corridor Gazing

Lining up for assembly, Utsav's head was turned 90 degrees, tracking Aditi in the parallel line. He almost hit a pillar until Didi snapped, "Eyes front!" Aditi hadn't noticed.

The Lab Coat Adjustment

In the lab, Aditi's bag strap slipped. Utsav instinctively reached to catch it, hand hovering gently before pulling back. Aditi adjusted it herself, walking away. Didi saw the longing in his eyes, realizing he was learning the hard lessons of one-sided affection.

August brought Independence Day fervor. Gupta Sir cast Utsav as the Chief Minister for the coaching center's skit. Utsav rehearsed his speech in an oversized Nehru jacket for hours.

But relentless monsoon rains flooded the stage. The program was postponed to Republic Day.

This triggered a crisis. It was 2012, the year of the Maya Calendar Prophecy predicting the world's end in December.

"Sir," a senior asked. "If the world ends in December, how can we perform in January?"

Utsav sat wide-eyed. If the world ended, he only had four months left to tell Aditi she was the love of his life. Armed with doomsday courage, he decided to confess. But the universe wrote a comedy.

The "Last Wish" Blunder

"Aditi, the world is ending," Utsav said solemnly.

"My dad says it's fake news," she chewed her lunch.

"But if we only had one day left, what is the one thing you want to know?" He was ready to scream "ME!" if she asked who loved her.

"I want to know if Anshu actually cheated or if she is really that smart." His romantic balloon popped.

The "Kneeling" Misunderstanding Utsav dropped to one knee in the corridor. Before he could speak, Aditi looked down concerned. "Did your contact lens fall out? Or a coin?" She bent to search. Face burning, Utsav pretended to look for an eraser.

The "Main Tumse..." Panic

Blocking her path at the water cooler, he took a deep breath. "Main tumse..." (*I want to tell you...*) Aditi waited. Fear paralyzed him. "...Main tumse... Geometry Box maangne aaya tha. Do you have a compass?" (*I came to ask for a Geometry box.*)

"Why do you need a compass for English?" she frowned.

"For... underlining nouns," he blurted. She gave him a weird look, handed it over, and left.

December 31, 2012. Utsav watched the clock, terrified he would die a ghost who never proposed.

12:01 AM. January 1, 2013.

The world survived. The timeline was safe.

As Republic Day approached, Gupta Sir asked Utsav which role he wanted in the school play. Thinking the title of Chief Minister sounded powerful enough to impress Aditi, Utsav accepted the part instantly without ever reading the script.

But reality hit hard when the pages were finally handed out. Five lines. A mere cameo at the very end to deliver a vote of thanks.

"Is this just the summary?" Utsav asked, staring at the single piece of paper.

"That is the entire role," Gupta Sir chuckled. "You are free to roam while the others rehearse."

Utsav felt humiliated, ready to throw the script away. But Aadil Bhaiya, who had returned to the school grounds to direct the Republic Day performances, placed a heavy hand on his shoulder.

"A five-line script is a weapon, Utsav," Aadil Bhaiya said, his charismatic voice commanding instant respect. "Amateurs need a hundred pages to make the audience cry. A true actor only needs five seconds. Don't just read the words. Make those five lines bleed."

Freedom to roam meant nothing if he couldn't find Aditi. Spotting her under the Neem tree, he prepared his approach, but his friend Shyam dragged him away for samosas. By the time Utsav rushed back, the bench was empty.

He chased a flash of her white uniform straight into the Singing Room. It was an ocean of girls, absolute social suicide for a boy. He almost retreated until he spotted his classmate Shahid holding a harmonium.

"Shahid, I want to sing too," Utsav declared.

"This is traditional classical. You need to know the Sur and Taal," Shahid replied seriously. "Auditions are closed anyway."

Utsav's face fell. Aditi was sitting right in the front row, clutching her lyrics.

The Singing Teacher walked in and paused. "Arey, Utsav! Do you want to eat the careers of the singers now? You are already the topper and the drama star. Leave something for us untalented folks!"

The room erupted in laughter. Utsav's eyes darted instantly to Aditi. She was laughing.

Time stopped. *She is laughing, and I am the reason.* It was a warm, electric high.

"So, Utsav," the teacher asked, wiping a tear. "I have never seen you sing. When exactly do you practice?"

Utsav looked at him deadpan. "I practice daily, Sir. When I am under the shower."

The room exploded. Aditi laughed so hard she dropped her lyric sheet, looking up at him with pure intrigue. He walked out feeling ten feet tall.

January 12, 2013. The School Ground.

The cast and crew of the Republic Day play were sitting in a large, messy circle on the grass, taking a break from Aadil Bhaiya's intense rehearsal. Sweaters were unbuttoned, and lunchboxes were open.

Navya: *(Carefully packing her perfectly clean tiffin box)* "I am just so relieved we are actually sitting here practicing for the 26th of January. A month ago, I was genuinely preparing my soul for the end of the world."

Aditi: *(Hugging her knees, looking completely serious)* "Don't even laugh, Navya. I was terrified. On December 21st, I literally couldn't sleep. Every time a truck drove heavily on the highway, I thought the earth was cracking open. I spent the whole night staring at the ceiling, waiting for the Mayan calendar to just delete us."

Shyam: *(Stuffed with half a samosa in his mouth)* "I was terrified too, Aditi! Do you know how much anxiety I had? I realized that if the world ended at midnight, I would die without eating the paneer pakoras my mom was supposed to make for breakfast. I literally forced her to fry them at 10 PM. If I was going down, I was going down full."

Kamal: *(Laughing)* "Shyam, the apocalypse could happen right now and you'd still ask the meteor if it brought chutney."

Rajat: *(Dusting off his imported wool sweater with a smug smile)* "You guys panic like peasants. It was obviously a hoax, but even if it wasn't, my dad was prepared. He imported this thermal-insulated survival tent from Germany. It can withstand sub-zero temperatures and earthquakes. If the world ended, the Ether Enclave residents would have just camped out in luxury."

Paridhi: *(Rolling her eyes)* "Yes, Rajat. The world exploding into a ball of fire would definitely respect your German tent."

Muskan: *(Smirking and tossing a peanut at Tejas)* "Exactly. Rajat's tent would have flown straight to the moon. Right, Tejas? Or did you plan to stop the 2012 tsunami by throwing your thick history textbook at the water?"

Tejas: *(Adjusting his glasses, completely serious)* "Actually, Muskan, Chronos is geographically safe from tsunamis because we are landlocked. The most probable doomsday scenario for Uttar Pradesh would have been a tectonic shift causing a massive earthquake along the fault lines."

Muskan: *(Slow clapping)* "Wow. The Mayans are shaking in their graves. Tejas just cancelled the apocalypse with geography. The meteor saw Tejas standing there with an atlas and decided to turn around."

The group bursts into laughter. Utsav, sitting quietly beside Shyam, smiles but keeps tracing the grass with a twig.

Aditi: *(Turning to the group, pointing at Utsav)* "You know who acted the weirdest during the whole 2012 thing? Utsav. On the last day, he literally walked up to me in the corridor, looking like a tragic movie hero, and said, *'Aditi, the world is ending. What is your last wish?'* I swear, he looked like he was about to magically grant it!"

Everyone turns to Utsav. Shyam tries to hide a massive grin, knowing exactly why Utsav had asked that question.

Utsav: *(Without missing a beat, looking up with a lazy, witty smirk)* "Well, I was fully prepared to do something profound. But since you wasted your absolute *last* wish on earth asking me if Anshu's cheating in exams rumors were true... I figured the universe was so disappointed by your lack of imagination that it decided to keep spinning just to annoy me."

Shyam: *(Roaring with laughter and slapping Utsav's back)* "Oh my god! You asked him about Anshu?! Aditi, you are obsessed!"

Aditi: *(Blushing a deep red, swatting at Shyam)* "It was a valid question! The world was ending, I needed closure!"

Muskan: *(Leaning forward, suddenly curious)* "Wait, speaking of closure, I have a genuine question. Why did everyone think it was specifically December 21, 2012? Who actually came up with that exact date?"

Tejas: *(Clearing his throat, switching to his 'Class Historian' voice)* "It's based on the Mesoamerican Long Count calendar. December 21 marked the end of a 5,126-year-long cycle called the 13th Baktun. It wasn't actually an apocalypse prophecy; it was just the calendar resetting, like our December 31st."

Muskan: *(Staring at Tejas deadpan)* "So you're telling me... the whole world had a collective panic attack, news channels ran 24/7 coverage, and Shyam ate midnight pakoras... all because an ancient civilization basically forgot to buy a new calendar from the stationery shop?"

Kamal: *(Wheezing)* "They ran out of paper!"

Priti: *(Tucking a loose strand of hair behind her ear, looking down shyly but making sure everyone notices her wrist)* "I mean... I know it sounds silly now. But I was a little scared. So on the 20th, I just decided to wear the new diamond-studded watch my uncle brought from London, and the pure Pashmina shawl my mom got. I just sat on the sofa looking at them. I figured... if the world ends, at least I should look elegant when I go."

Muskan: *(Whispering loudly to Gauri)* "If a volcano erupts, Priti's last words will be asking the lava not to ruin her branded shoes."

Navya: *(Shaking her head, clutching her perfectly maintained script)* "You all are crazy. Do you want to know what I did on December 20th? I finished my entire winter holiday homework. All of it. Math, Science, and Hindi."

Rajat: *(Staring at her)* "Why would you do homework if the world was going to end?"

Navya: *(Adjusting her collar, looking terrified at the mere thought)* "Because! What if the world *didn't* end, and Gupta Sir decided to check our copies on the 1st of January? A meteor hitting the earth is fine, but getting scolded by Gupta Sir for incomplete homework? That is a real doomsday."

Utsav: *(Laughing softly, tossing his twig away)* "Navya is the only one here with actual survival instincts. The Mayans are gone, but Gupta Sir's red pen is eternal."

Shyam: *(Standing up and dusting his pants)* "Well, the world didn't end. Which means we still have to perform this play, and I still have to die in Utsav's arms on stage. Speaking of which, Utsav, if you drop me during the climax on the 26th, I will personally restart the Mayan calendar."

Utsav: *(Smiling, his eyes briefly catching Aditi's)* "Don't worry, Shyam. I won't let you fall."

January 26, 2013.

The play reached its violent climax. A shooter emerged, and the young patriot leaped in front of the Chief Minister, taking the bullet. The crowd gasped.

Utsav stepped forward. He remembered Aadil Bhaiya's intense backstage coaching: *Drop the volume. Make them lean in. Let the silence do the heavy lifting.* Kneeling beside the fallen hero, Utsav didn't shout. His voice rang out heavy, trembling with raw, calculated emotion.

"He did not take a bullet for a man. He took a bullet for Democracy. The blood on this floor is not red; it is Tricolour. We sleep because he bled. We live because he died. Jai Hind."

Five lines. A stunned, pin-drop silence swept the ground, instantly followed by a thunderous roar. Just as Aadil Bhaiya had promised, Utsav's five seconds completely overshadowed the entire hour-long play.

Later, he returned without a costume to recite his self-composed poem about Veer Savarkar's escape from Cellular Jail.

"The night was silent, the guards were asleep, I surrendered my soul to the ocean deep. Let the ocean try to drown my plea, You can chain the man, but not the sea."

A tear rolled down the Principal's cheek. The Chief Guest handed Utsav an on-the-spot cash prize of five hundred rupees. But Utsav only looked for Aditi, who was clapping in absolute awe.

Utsav delivered the Closing Speech, turning the wooden podium into a pulpit. "If Savarkar could swim the ocean with chains, can we not swim through our syllabus?"

The crowd was on the edge of their seats. The applause was deafening. Walking down the steps, he saw Aditi looking at him with undeniable pride. He felt like the absolute King of the World, having conquered the stage entirely for his Muse.

Standing near the refreshment stall, Utsav tasted the sweet victory of a Boondi Laddu. But as he took the second bite, reality hit him harder than a math problem.

March.

The Final Exams were a month away. While Utsav was busy being the Chief Minister, reciting poems, and swimming in Aditi's admiration, the syllabus had piled up like a mountain. Mentally, he had been busy writing mental poetry for her.

He realized he had made a classic mistake: The Topper's Dilemma.

In Vidya International School, an unwritten rule stated that "Real Toppers" didn't dance. They believed rehearsals stole time from revision and viewed the stage as a distraction.

But Utsav and Aditi were different. They believed school was also about Personality. Standing on a stage built courage textbooks couldn't teach.

But popularity doesn't write exam papers.

Utsav finished his laddu, spotting Aditi near the water cooler. "Aditi," he asked with sudden urgency. "How is the prep going? Are you ready to leave Anshu behind?"

Aditi smiled dismissively. "Honestly? I have been observing Anshu. I think she has given up. She doesn't raise her hand anymore. She looks exhausted. There is no point in defeating someone who has already walked out of the ring, right?"

Aditi made a fatal error. She confused silence with surrender. She didn't know the silence of a tiger is an ambush.

Two days later, the illusion shattered during a Physics period. Mr. Verma conducted a surprise oral test on an untaught chapter.

"Who can tell me the relationship between the coefficient of friction and the angle of repose?"

The class went silent. Then, a hand went up slowly, lazily. It was Anshu.

She stood up with the boredom of a genius. "Sir, the angle of repose is equal to the angle of friction. Therefore, the coefficient of friction is equal to the tangent of the angle of repose..."

Mr. Verma looked stunned. "That is correct. But how do you know this?"

Anshu looked around, her eyes lingering on Aditi for a fraction of a second—a cold, calculated look.

"Because, Sir," Anshu said, closing her book. "While everyone was practicing for the dance and memorizing poems, I finished the entire syllabus of Class 5. Twice."

She sat down. Deafening silence. Aditi turned pale.

Anshu hadn't stepped back. She had stepped away from distractions to sharpen her knife in the dark. She had built a lead that was mathematically impossible to cover.

Utsav looked at Aditi's terrified face. *The Chief Minister speech won't save us now. The war has just begun.*

Anshu's answer was a declaration of war. Before turning back to the blackboard, she did something that unsettled the class even more. She turned her head slightly and looked directly at Utsav.

The message was clear: *You played the Chief Minister. I played the student. Now watch who rules.*

Aditi sat frozen in a whirlpool of emotions. Terrified by the canyon-like gap between her and Anshu, a twisted smile still touched her lips. Defeating a weak Anshu would have been boring. *She is still the monster,* Aditi thought, adrenaline replacing fear.

But why did Anshu reveal her preparation now? Was it arrogance, or a psychological tactic to break Aditi's confidence?

While Aditi dealt with fear, Utsav dealt with an impossible equation. He had 28 Days left. He was trapped.

Scenario A: If Utsav studies with his full potential, he crushes everyone. Result: Utsav 1st, Anshu 2nd, Aditi 3rd. *Outcome: Aditi is sad. Utsav fails as a lover.*

Scenario B: If Utsav sabotages himself, he drops marks. But Anshu is prepared. Result: Anshu 1st, Aditi 2nd, Utsav 3rd. *Outcome: Aditi loses the crown. Anshu wins. Utsav fails as a protector.*

"What do I do?" Utsav whispered. He couldn't win, and he couldn't let her lose. The margin for error was zero.

For the first time, Utsav realized loving a competitor is the hardest thing in the world. You want them to win, but they can only win if you lose—yet you have to be good enough to catch them if they fall.

February arrived with the "Ghost Mode" of Class 5-A. Aditi and Utsav became machines.

Aditi stopped looking at the Neem tree. She woke at 4 AM and studied until midnight, fueled by fear of Anshu's knowledge, devouring textbooks for hidden facts.

Utsav watched the dark circles under Aditi's eyes. He decided to stop calculating and start working. *I will be so prepared that if Aditi needs help, I can teach her. I will be her backup generator.*

He went back to studying line-by-line, memorizing dates and solving difficult Math problems. Conversations between them stopped completely. There was only the scratching of pens and suffocating pressure. They were two soldiers preparing to fight a dragon named Anshu.

The Final Exams arrived. Utsav walked into the hall and went to Aditi's aisle seat.

"Aditi," he whispered. "You are not alone in this battle. I am with you."

He laid out the plan. "In every paper, mark the keywords you write. After every exam, we will reconcile the numbers. We will calculate exactly how much you are scoring."

"Why are you putting so much strategy into this?" Aditi frowned.

"If we are in competition with Anshu, we move with calculation. I want you to come on Top. I will be Second."

"Why aren't you desiring to top? You are the genius."

"I don't want to be the center of attraction," Utsav scoffed. He paused, looking her dead in the eye. "I want you to top... because you are so beautiful."

Aditi blinked. "What?"

Utsav froze. "I mean... you are beautifully intelligent! Clever. You deserve to be on top."

Aditi narrowed her eyes, smiling. "No. You said 'I am so beautiful.' Tell me."

Utsav sighed. "You are the most beautiful girl in the entire school. It would be a great combination if you also top the class. Beauty with Brains."

Aditi blushed a deep, rosy pink. "You are such a mystery, Utsav."

The exams began. They would meet at the Neem tree to audit her performance. On the last day, Utsav did the math. Aditi's expected score: 587. His own, even with penalties: 588 to 594.

He was winning. If he scored normally in the last exam, Aditi would be Second or Third. The plan would fail.

The final paper was unique: Physical Education & Singing (100 Marks). 50 marks for singing, 50 marks for appearance (uniform, shoes, socks, nails, etc.).

Aditi would be perfect. She would score 50/50 in PE and sing beautifully. Utsav realized he had to sabotage his appearance.

On the morning of the exam, Utsav arrived late deliberately to execute his "Swag" entry.

"May I come in..." The word died in his throat.

Sitting in the teacher's chair was Badi Didi.

Utsav's heart stopped. His own sister was the invigilator for the "Uniform Inspection." *She should not see my feet,* his mind screamed.

Badi Didi practiced strict Auditor's Professional Ethics. Utsav was just Roll Number 23 inside these walls.

"Yeah, come in," she said flatly.

Utsav scurried along the wall, hiding his lower half, and threw himself onto the last bench, pulling his legs deep under the desk. If Didi saw his feet, he would lose marks (good) but get a lecture at home (bad).

Aditi was staring out the window in horror. Vice Principal Sir, the "Discipline In-charge," was outside whacking a student's calves with a bamboo stick. The whole class flinched.

While Aditi stared at the violence outside, Utsav sat terrified of the silence inside, caught between the love that made him sabotage his uniform and the sister waiting to grade him.

"Roll Number One!" Badi Didi called. Preeti, the princess of Panchvati, opted out of singing, whispered a poem, secured her 35 marks, and sat down.

"Roll Number Two!" Anshu sang "Ambarsariya" strongly. The applause was deafening, largely from the Vijay Chowk Gang. It was a turf war.

"Roll Number Three... Aditi."

Aditi stood up. If angels have a dress code, she wore it. She looked like a guardian angel in her uniform, her double ponytails acting as halos woven from midnight silk.

Utsav giggled into his desk. *Didi is about to meet her Sister-in-Law.* Aditi began to sing "Tose naina laage." In the middle, she transitioned into a complex classical Aalaap. Her voice was crystal clear, holding the room in a trance.

When she finished, even strict Badi Didi was impressed. "Aditi," Didi said warmly. "You are an outperformer. And... you are so beautiful also. If I had the power, I would give you unlimited marks."

Utsav's chest swelled. He scribbled Didi's words on the desk wood. *The approval is granted.* The class erupted in cheers.

Then Didi raised her hand. "Silence! Roll Number Four... Utsav."

Utsav's heart stopped. The floor felt like lava. He stood up slowly.

Usually, the walk of a topper is the heavy thud of polished leather. But Utsav's walk sounded different. *Squeak... squish... squeak.* The sound of rubber.

Aditi heard the sound and looked at his feet. A jolt of shock ran through her. She slapped her forehead in frustration. *Why? Why is he handing me the sword? Does he think I can't win? Or... does he just want me to shine?*

Anshu was equally frozen. She had prepared for war, expecting Utsav to fight for every decimal point. This was voluntary surrender. She realized Utsav was playing a game with no rules and no logic.

Utsav reached the front. Badi Didi looked down. Her eyes widened.

He was wearing loud, Neon Purple Sports Shoes. A flag waving in the administration's face, begging for deductions.

Didi's face shifted through shock, rage, and confusion, until she saw Utsav's suppressed grin and twinkling eyes.

"Utsav," she asked dangerously low. "You didn't wear the black shoes."

"No, Ma'am. They were unpolished."

"There was polish in the cupboard."

"Mice took that away," Utsav lied confidently.

"At least you should have worn socks."

"No, Ma'am. A mouse had bitten the bottom of the feet. I cannot risk the integrity of the uniform check."

Didi rubbed her teeth together. "Zero for Shoes. Zero for Socks. Show your nails."

Utsav extended his hands. He was a chronic nail-biter, but today his nails were long, untrimmed growth. Didi gasped, realizing the dedication it took to let them grow just to fail today.

"You have claws? What is going on?"

"Ma'am, these are my personal agenda. You are only required to grade the result."

Didi hid a smile. "Sing," she commanded.

He chose "Jeene Laga Hoon" (I have started living). He wasn't singing to the class; he was singing to Aditi.

"Pehle se zyada... tumpe marne laga hoon..." (More than before... I am dying for you...)

Aditi realized this charade wasn't about failing; it was about living. He was telling her that her victory meant more to him than his reputation.

Badi Didi hid her laughter behind the register. She finally understood. He was engineering his score to be exactly Second.

Utsav finished. Anshu and Aditi clapped first. Aditi clapped with a ferocity that surprised everyone, her shining eyes acknowledging the boy who had painted his feet purple to make her a Queen.

The atmosphere shifted to competitive desperation. PE was the "Jackpot Subject" for free marks. Everyone was eager to perform.

Then it was Shyam's turn. Utsav's loyal best friend walked to the front confidently.

"Sing."

"Poem, Ma'am," Shyam puffed out his chest.

"Hua savera chidiya boli... Achhe bachche manjan karte..." (Morning has come... Good children brush their teeth...)

Heavy silence followed. Then, the entire Class 5-A slapped their foreheads. *Smack.* Didi was confused. "Shyam... is this a joke?"

Tejas, the class historian, stood up, laughing. "Ma'am. It is a legacy. Shyam learned this poem in UKG. In Class 1, Class 3, Class 4 Quarterly, Half-Yearly, Final... he recited 'Hua Savera Chidiya Boli'."

Tejas threw his hands up. "Now we are in Class 5 Finals. We learned Algebra. And Shyam is still brushing his teeth! Dude! The birds have flown away! Change the poem!"

Badi Didi cracked. The strict Invigilator threw her head back and laughed hard. The class erupted, laughing at Shyam's sheer consistency and innocence amidst competitive tension.

Shyam grinned sheepishly. He didn't mind; he had secured his passing marks.

In that roaring laughter, exam stress evaporated. Utsav looked at Aditi laughing, then at Shyam. While he and Aditi were writing a complex love story, Shyam was living a simple comedy. And sometimes, *'Hua Savera Chidiya Boli'* was exactly what the heart needed.

The moment Utsav stepped inside his house after the last exam, the storm broke. Badi Didi hadn't forgotten; she had merely delayed the execution. The living room was converted into a courtroom.

The Judge: Papa. The Prosecutor: Badi Didi. The Jury: Mummy and Dadaji. The Accomplice: Chhoti Didi. The Accused: Utsav.

Badi Didi threw her bag on the sofa. "Mummy! Do you know what your 'Laadla' did today? In the Final Exam! In front of the whole school!"

"What happened?" Mummy wiped her hands. "Did he leave the paper blank?"

"Worse! It was the Uniform Inspection. 50 marks! And this boy walks in wearing Purple Sports Shoes! And look at his nails! He looks like a werewolf!"

Mummy’s eyes widened. "Purple shoes? Utsav, where were your black shoes?"

Utsav looked at the floor. "Mummy, the mice..."

"Stop!" Badi Didi snapped. "Don't you dare repeat that mice story here. Papa, he told me mice ate the shoe polish and bit holes in his socks. He lied to a teacher!"

Papa looked up from his newspaper, his voice calm but stern. "Utsav. Is this true? Did you lie about the mice?"

"Papa... I just... the black shoes were really tight. My feet were hurting." A new excuse.

"Oh? And the nails? Was the nail cutter also eaten by a tiger?" Badi Didi glared. "He had 4mm long nails, Papa! I had to give him a Zero. A straight Zero!"

Chhoti Didi tried to save him. "Didi, maybe he just forgot. And those purple shoes... I gifted them. They are nice, right?"

Badi Didi glared at her. "This is your fault too. You spoil him. Who wears party shoes to an exam?"

Mummy twisted Utsav's ear gently but firmly. "I ironed your uniform last night. I kept the black shoes ready. You changed them on purpose? Why? Do you want to fail?"

Utsav stood silent. He couldn't tell them, *I wanted to fail so the girl I love could win.*

Dadaji cleared his throat. "Okay, okay. The exam is over. He got a Zero, right? Punishment received. Now leave the boy alone. Maybe he wanted to stand out." Dadaji looked at Utsav with a knowing twinkle. "Or maybe... he had his own reasons. A man doesn't destroy his own house without a reason."

The tribunal was dismissed, but Utsav got a strict warning: Next time, if the uniform isn't perfect, the purple shoes will be burned.

A few days later, the "Auditor" left. Badi Didi packed her bags for her own graduation exams in Radiance, a city 150 kilometers from Chronos where Bhaiya lived.

"Study for the next session," she warned Utsav before leaving. "And cut those nails."

With her gone, the house felt lighter, but Utsav missed his shield. However, he had bigger things to worry about: March 31, 2013. Result Day.

The Golden Gap (March 20–30, 2013)

With exams over and Badi Didi away, the "Strict Government" fell, and the "Democratic Republic of Utsav and Chhoti Didi" was established.

Chhoti Didi was four years older—the "Sweet Spot" of sibling relationships. She wasn't a second mother, nor a nuisance. She was his partner-in-crime, secret keeper, and best friend.

Those ten days held many untold stories:

The 9XM Wars

Lazy afternoons turned the living room into a battlefield. Utsav wanted Cricket Highlights; Chhoti Didi wanted Songs on 9XM.

"Remote de!" Utsav yelled, trying to snatch it.

"Nahi! *Badtameez Dil* aa raha hai!" Chhoti Didi screamed, holding the remote high above her head.

The compromise was always the same: Songs won. They would sit sharing a bowl of chips. When *Jeene Laga Hoon* played, Chhoti Didi would nudge Utsav.

"Oye, Hero," she would tease, pulling his cheek. "Yeh gaana kiske liye gaaya tha exam mein? Sach bata?" (Who did you sing this for? Tell the truth.)

Utsav would blush, hiding his face in a cushion. "Kisi ke liye nahi. Bas marks ke liye." (No one. Just for marks.)

"Jhootha," (Liar) she laughed. "You wore my purple shoes to impress her by failing, right?"

Utsav looked at her, shocked. She knew. She always knew. And she never told Mummy. That was their deal.

The Midnight Maggi Ritual

Since Utsav was "The Man with the Money," he felt generous. One night at 11 PM, he poked her arm. "Didi, bhookh lagi hai." (I'm hungry.)

Chhoti Didi pretended to be annoyed but got up immediately. They tiptoed to the kitchen, where she made the dry, spicy Maggi only siblings know how to make perfectly. They sat on the kitchen slab, eating from the same pot to avoid noise.

"Didi," Utsav asked, blowing on a hot forkful. "Do you think I will come Second?"

Chhoti Didi stopped eating. She wiped a smudge of masala from his chin. "Tu Second aaye ya Last," she said softly, "Tu sabse smart hai. And honestly? Those purple shoes looked cool."

Utsav grinned. Sharing noodles in the quiet kitchen, he realized that while Aditi was his crush, Chhoti Didi was his anchor.

The Nail Salon

On March 25th, the crisis of the nails had to be addressed. They were still 4mm long, jagged, and annoying.

"Bring the cutter," Chhoti Didi commanded. Sitting in the evening sun, she carefully clipped his nails one by one, filing the rough edges so he wouldn't scratch himself.

"Why do you bite them, Utsav?" she asked gently.

"Stress," Utsav muttered. "Thinking about... everything."

"Mat socha kar," she tapped his nose. "Jab tak main hoon, tujhe stress lene ki zaroorat nahi hai. Main hoon na Badi Didi se bachane ke liye." (Don't think. As long as I am here, you don't need to stress. I am here to save you from Badi Didi.)

It was a small moment, showing the depth of their dependency. She groomed him, protected him, and made him presentable.

The Saree Experiment

Chhoti Didi wanted to practice wearing a saree for a school farewell but lacked a full-length mirror. Draping Mummy's red saree over her jeans, she asked, "Utsav, batana kaisi lag rahi hoon." (Tell me how I look.)

Utsav acted as fashion judge. "Pleats theek nahi hain. Left side se neeche hai." (Pleats aren't right. Lower on the left.)

She fixed it. "Ab?" (Now?)

"Better. But you look like Mummy's younger version."

She beamed and started dancing to the radio. Utsav joined her with his clumsy "Chief Minister" steps. They danced like maniacs, laughing until their stomachs hurt, tripping over the pallu.

The Bank of Trust

On March 29th, Utsav took out his stash of Dakshina notes. "Didi, count karwa do."

They counted together. "You worked really hard for this, na? Mantra yaad karne mein?" she asked.

"Haan," Utsav nodded.

"Proud of you, Bhai," she messed up his hair. "You are buying your own admission. Even I haven't done that yet."

She didn't ask for a share or a treat. She looked at him with pure pride. Silently, Utsav tucked two □100 notes into her palm.

"Yeh kya hai?" she asked.

"Commission," Utsav winked. "For keeping the Purple Shoe secret."

She laughed and hugged him tight. Those ten days bridged their childhoods. They fought over the TV, shared secrets, ate from the same plate, and protected each other. Utsav was chasing Aditi's heart, but a huge chunk of his own belonged to Chhoti Didi.

The "Spikes" Disaster

In 2013, "Spiked Hair" was the ultimate fashion statement. Utsav wanted the Ranbir Kapoor look to impress Aditi. Water and soap failed to hold his hair up.

"Didi! Mujhe spikes chahiye!" he shouted.

Chhoti Didi walked in eating an apple. "I have a secret formula. Bhaiya uses it."

She mixed sugar and water, applying the sticky syrup to Utsav's hair, pulling it into rock-hard spikes. He felt electric.

He went to the terrace to dry it. The problem: Sugar attracts bees and flies. Within 10 minutes, flies buzzed around his sweet head, and a bee tried to land.

Utsav ran screaming, "Didi! Madhumakkhi!"

Chhoti Didi laughed until she fell on the bed, while Utsav washed his head three times. He learned that beauty involves pain, but sticky hair involves insects.

The Holi War 2013

Utsav hated "Pakka Rang" (permanent paint). He locked himself in his room. "Main Holi nahi khelunga!"

Chhoti Didi waited outside with a bucket of silver paint and oil. "Utsav, bahar nikal! Aaj Holi hai!"

"Nahi! I have allergies!" he lied.

She used the ultimate weapon: "If you don't come out, I will tell Mummy about the 'Love Letter' practice notes in your Geometry box."

The door opened instantly. "Face pe mat lagana, please."

She smirked, hugged him, said "Happy Holi, Bhai," and splashed him. He looked like a Silver Alien. Handing him a water gun, she said, "Now let's go attack Bhaiya." They spent two hours terrorizing the neighborhood. Later, she spent an hour scrubbing his face with coconut oil so he wouldn't look like a statue.

The "English-Only" Challenge

Bored, they decided to be "Posh."

"From now on, we will speak only in English for one hour," Chhoti Didi announced. "No Hindi. Fine is □10."

"Challenge accepted," Utsav agreed.

"Sister, the sun is very... burning today."

"Yes. The heat is doing too much."

"I want to eat... umm... Water-Balls (Pani Puri)."

"Water balls are hygienic not. Eat biscuits."

Silence followed as they ran out of vocabulary. Then, a street dog chased a cat into their garden.

"Arey hat! Kutta aa gaya! Bhaga usko!" Utsav shouted.

"Hindi! La 10 rupaye!" she pointed.

"No! Even dogs don't understand English in India. It was necessary translation!" They argued in Hindi for 20 minutes about the linguistic capabilities of dogs.

The Last Shield (The Dog Incident)

Days before the tragedy, Utsav played outside, swinging a stick like a sword. The street dogs saw a threat. Four dogs chased him. Panic made his little legs clumsy; he tripped and fell hard. A dog nipped his calf, drawing blood.

He limped home screaming. Mummy was furious, her fear looking like anger. "Why did you provoke them? Now we need injections!"

Utsav trembled, terrified of the pain and her anger. Chhoti Didi stepped between them. "Mummy, bas. He didn't provoke them. The dogs were aggressive today." It was a lie, but her brother needed a defender.

She took the cotton, cleaning his wound gently. "Dard ho raha hai?"

Utsav nodded, crying.

"Sher bachhe rote nahi," she wiped his tears. "Main hoon na. Kuch nahi hoga."

She was his shield against fear and pain. No one knew the shield itself was breaking from the inside.

The Night Before the Result (March 30)

Utsav tossed and turned, peaking with anxiety. Chhoti Didi sat on his bed. "Darr lag raha hai? What if Anshu beats me?"

She didn't lecture; she hummed *'Give me some sunshine...'* from *3 Idiots*. Utsav joined in softly.

"Tu tension mat le," she patted his head. "Topper tu hi hai. And if not, you are still 'Pandit'. We will open a temple together."

Utsav laughed. The fear melted away. He fell asleep holding her hand, knowing he had the best support system in the world.

Result Day
31st march 2013

The school hall was packed. The air was thick with tension for the conclusion of the "Cold War" between the Highway, Vijay Chowk, and the posh colonies.

The Principal took the mic. "In the history of Vidya International School, we have never seen a competition this close. The difference between the Top 3 is not of intelligence, but of destiny."

"Rank 3... goes to Anshu. With 678/700."

Anshu froze. 678. She had studied the syllabus twice, yet she lost. The pain was realizing that despite being perfect, she wasn't the best.

"Rank 2... goes to Utsav. With 679/700."

Utsav exhaled. He had beaten Anshu by 1 mark. His strategy of "Controlled Failure" had worked with terrifying precision. He landed exactly where he wanted—the prince guarding the Queen.

"And Rank 1... The Topper of Class 5... is Aditi. With 686/700."

The hall erupted. 686. Aditi had done it, reclaiming her throne by a solid margin. Her eyes filled with tears of relief.

Utsav clapped the hardest. *Calculated risk,* he thought. *Mission Accomplished.*

After the ceremony, the administrative counter was crowded with parents paying fees for Class 6. Utsav saw Aditi's well-dressed father hand over a thick bundle of cash, a display of stability.

Utsav stood in line behind him, alone, clutching a small cloth bag.

Vice Principal Sir looked down at him. "Utsav? Where is your mother?"

"She is at home. I have come to submit the fees."

"You? It is a large amount."

"I know, Sir." Utsav pulled out a stack of 50s, 100s, 500s, and 1000s. They smelled of flowers. He fumbled with the thick bundle, looking like a child struggling with a brick of gold.

Vice Principal Sir's eyes widened. He knew Utsav's family was well-off. But seeing a Class 5 student with thousands of rupees was shocking.

This wasn't pocket money. This was *Dakshina.*

Utsav's Dadaji had taught him the ancient art of Priesthood rituals. During holidays, while others played, Utsav learned Sanskrit Mantras. Recently, he had flawlessly assisted in a grand Rudrabhishek, and the impressed hosts gave him a generous share. Utsav saved every rupee to be independent.

"Count it, Sir. It is for my re-admission and fees."

Vice Principal Sir counted. It was exact. "Receipt le lo," he said softly.

Utsav felt a different pride today. Aditi's father paid for her because he loved her. Utsav paid for himself to be worthy of standing next to her in maturity.

Utsav was not poor. His father was an Inventory Manager, his mother ran a sewing center, his Bhaiya was a genius MBA/CA student, Badi Didi was a teacher, and Dadaji was a revered figure. Utsav was the "Laadla" (beloved). If he had asked for fees, his mother would have given them instantly. But Utsav had Self-Respect.

The morning of April 1st smelled of starch. Utsav stood in front of the mirror wearing his crisp new uniform—armor bought with *Dakshina*. His admission was a trust placed in him by the administration, and he had to prove he was worth it.

"Utsav," his Grandfather called. "You will be late."

He touched his feet and stepped out onto the Chronicle-Nectar Highway. Vidya International School stood 70 meters away. Crossing the highway, he entered the sprawling campus. Rich kids from posh enclaves stepped out of SUVs. Utsav felt invisible, yet exposed.

He found Class 6-A. It was a massive room crammed with nearly 100 students from the combined 5-A and 5-B sections. Groups were already solidified. The Zenith Group (Aditi, Muskan) sat in the middle, glowing with intelligence. The Ojas Enclave Gang (Shyam) occupied the back. The Ether Enclave Traders (Zaid, Rajat) gathered near the window.

Utsav knew no one. The "New Admission." He sat quietly in the third row, keeping his bag on his lap.

During the assembly, Shyam joked, "Don't worry, the Principal talks for thirty minutes. You can sleep standing up."

"Shyam, keep quiet! The prayer is starting," Aditi shushed him from the girls' line.

Utsav looked at her perfect posture and closed eyes. *Rank 1,* his mind guessed.

During recess, Utsav sat alone, watching class dynamics. He opened his notebook and wrote his ambition: *To be the best.* He didn't know that soon, a phone call would shatter his world, testing his "Dakshina" admission with tragedy, and leaving his desk empty for three months. But today, he was a boy with a heart full of hope.

The new session began. Shyam was acting extremely weird.

"Bhai," Shyam struck a pose. "Hypothetically, if a girl wears white ribbons and looks like a fairy... how do we impress her?"

"Hypothetically," Utsav grinned, "tell her she looks like the moon."

Shyam blushed redder than a tomato and ran away giggling. Utsav didn't realize the "White Ribbon" description wasn't hypothetical.

April 2, 2013. During Morning Assembly, Shyam acted like a meerkat, craning his neck toward the Girls' Line—specifically where the sun hit Aditi's hair.

During recess by the water cooler, Shyam looked nervous. "Utsav. I can't hide it. I love her. Aditi."

Time froze. A lesser friend would have felt jealous. A possessive lover would have felt anger. *She is the Topper because I sacrificed my marks!* But Utsav was maturity personified. A genuine smile broke across his face. He put his arm around Shyam.

"Yaar Shyam. I admire your choice."

Shyam blinked. "You aren't angry? She is the Topper."

"She is the most beautiful girl in the world," Utsav said with pure devotion. "If you didn't love her, I'd think your eyes were broken. The fact that you like her proves our brotherhood. Great minds think alike."

"Doesn't it bother you that she is out of reach?"

"One-sided love is powerful, but only inside our heads. In reality, she exists. People will admire her. How can I stop the world from worshipping a goddess? We don't own her, Shyam. If my best friend loves her, it means he has the best taste."

Shyam smiled, relieved. Their friendship became complete.

Walking back, Utsav felt lighter. He realized love is not a cage. He believed in the Magnetic Law of Love: *If she is mine, she will return. If she doesn't, she never was.*

He didn't need to mark his territory. He was happy just knowing Aditi existed. He felt the wind, sunlight, and even the chalk dust were in love with her. She was so perfect that if Shyam or the world loved her, it was her fault, not theirs. You can't be jealous of the sun for shining; you just thank it.

Suddenly, a realization clicked.

He remembered Shyam dragging him away during lunch, discouraging him from acting in her play, and distracting him when Aditi looked his way.

Oh, Utsav realized. *He wasn't just being a friend. He was guarding the goalpost.* Shyam had been trying to minimize competition. But Utsav only felt sympathy. *Poor Shyam. He doesn't know that distances don't matter in love.* They were two soldiers fighting for the same kingdom—Shyam with strategy, Utsav with surrender.

But April 4 was approaching, and destiny was about to teach Utsav that losing a girl is nothing compared to losing a part of your soul.

God often weaves a cruel magic before calling someone back, bringing them closer than ever so their departure leaves a haunting echo.

Chhoti Didi's liver condition worsened rapidly. The Chronos doctors gave up, referring her to Radiance.

April 4, 2013. Utsav, Mummy, and Chhoti Didi boarded an overnight train to Radiance. Utsav loved the AC compartment.

From the upper berth, he looked down at weak, pale Chhoti Didi holding Mummy's hand.

"Goodnight, Didi," he whispered. She squeezed her eyes shut. He thought she was sleeping.

Morning light filtered through the blue-tinted windows. The train slowed. Utsav looked down and his blood froze.

Mummy was rocking back and forth, her face a mask of shattering shock. Chhoti Didi was still. Too still.

Utsav climbed down slowly. "Mummy?"

"Utsav," her voice sounded like broken glass. "Didi chali gayi." (Didi is gone.)

Utsav didn't scream or cry. He stood in the narrow aisle. The AC hummed. Outside, trees rushed by. Inside, death.

He looked at Chhoti Didi's peaceful face. Her hand rested on the sheet—the hand that had cut his nails, styled his hair, and cooked midnight Maggi.

How can she be gone? He felt a physical blow, sitting on the opposite berth, hugging his knees. He stared at her bare feet. *I should cover her feet. She will feel cold.* The world was moving. The sun was rising. But for Utsav, time stopped. He watched the lifeless body of his protector. The grief was a heavy, suffocating stone. His childhood died on that lower berth. The Shield was broken, and Utsav was terrifyingly alone.

April 5, 2013. 6:00 AM. The train halted at Lucknow. Indian Railways rules dictated dead bodies couldn't travel in passenger compartments. They were forced off.

On the cold, grey platform, tragedy was displayed. Mummy sat on the floor, stifling her screams, tears streaming down her face. Utsav sat on the other side of Chhoti Didi's wrapped body.

Utsav was sad, but also confused and irritated. *We have a confirmed AC ticket. Why did the Police Uncle make us get off?*

Everything he used to love about travel turned to poison.

The train tickets he obsessively collected now felt like trash—unable to save his sister.

The polished platform floors he loved sliding on in his Purple Shoes now felt like lead.

The platform stalls where he bought comics and snacks nauseated him, despite his pockets being full of *Dakshina*.

He used to love looking out at the rushing platform crowds from the cool AC coach. Now, he was in the crowd, and they were staring, whispering, "Body hai. Jawaan ladki thi." (It's a body. She was young.)

Why are you looking? he wanted to scream. The "VIP feeling" had turned into suffocation. The train was a metal box trapping them with death.

They hired a private Hearse Van to reach Radiance. Utsav loved road trips, but there was no music or snacks in the flat metal back.

Looking out the window, Utsav realized the trauma had rewired his brain. He hated the road, the train, the crowd, and the silence of the girl lying next to him.

Bhaiya arrived at Lucknow with a car. Seeing him provided a flicker of safety. Bhaiya arranged the hearse for Mummy and Chhoti Didi, but pulled Utsav onto his lap in the passenger seat of his car.

Usually, the front seat and Bhaiya's lap were ultimate luxuries. Today, Utsav hated the view of the road leading to a cremation. He buried his face in Bhaiya's chest, clinging to the only anchor keeping him from drowning.

In Radiance, Bhaiya detoured to his girlfriend's house. "You stay here for a while," he told Utsav softly.

Utsav didn't ask why. Bhaiya protected Utsav's eyes from the fire, ensuring his last memory of Chhoti Didi was her sleeping face, not ashes.

Hours later, a red-eyed Bhaiya took Utsav to the family home. The house was full—Papa, Mummy, Bhaiya, Badi Didi, Utsav. Usually, a full house meant joyful chaos. Today, the silence was a physical weight. The souls were broken.

Utsav realized the cruelty of cosmic balance. Bhaiya and Badi Didi were Team A. Chhoti Didi had felt lonely and prayed for a sibling. Utsav was her answered prayer—Team B.

Now, it felt like God had said, "I sent Utsav down to keep you company. Now I am calling you back." A soul-for-a-soul exchange. Utsav felt like a replacement that cost too much.

June 2, 2013. Bhaiya's Birthday. The family was still grieving, but brought a cake. Bhaiya looked down at Utsav. "Cake khilaoge Utsav?" (Will you feed me?)

For the first time in two months, a weak, genuine smile appeared on Utsav's lips. He fed Bhaiya a piece, and Bhaiya hugged him. Utsav realized Chhoti Didi had left him in the safest hands possible. Team B was broken, but Team A stepped down to hold him.

Laughter was forbidden, but Bhaiya used Commerce to manage Badi Didi's grief.

One night, Badi Didi cried over photos, refusing to eat. "Stop treating your tears like 'Revenue Expenditure'," Bhaiya said gently. "Treat this food like a 'Fixed Asset'. Depreciate it, generate energy, and give me some Return on Investment (ROI) by smiling."

Badi Didi chuckled. "You are such a nerd."

Utsav was confused. "Utsav, he means tears are useless spending, but food gives power. Commerce teaches us how to manage value," she explained. Commerce sounded like magic.

Later, when she regretted not seeing a doctor sooner, Bhaiya stopped her. "That is a 'Sunk Cost'. In Economics, we decide based on 'Opportunity Cost'. Your opportunity now is to look after Utsav. Don't let the Sunk Cost ruin the Future Venture."

Utsav liked how Bhaiya used logic to kill pain, learning that education wasn't just about marks—it was a way to understand life.

CHAPTER 4

Adyutsav: Lost inside own Castle

The mourning period ended. Reality called. June 20, 2013. Utsav returned to Chronos to rejoin Vidya International School.

But something was wrong. He felt like a stranger in his own kingdom.

From April 4 to June 20, Utsav hadn't touched a book. While his classmates ground through the rigorous Section A machine, he had been sitting in a hearse van, a train, and a grieving home.

Opening his books, the numbers looked like dancing spiders, the formulas like ancient hieroglyphs. The "Ranker Utsav" was gone, replaced by a traumatized boy whose memory was wiped clean by shock.

He was standing on a bicycle track while the class moved at the speed of a Ferrari. The syllabus had moved so far ahead he couldn't even see the other students' dust.

Vidya International School was a corporate strategy masterpiece designed by the Director's son, Nishant Sir. He operated the school on a "Formula 1 Timeline":

- **April - May (Aggressive Phase):** Complete 50% of the syllabus. No mercy.
- **Summer Vacation:** Revise the 50% and self-study the rest.
- **June - August:** Finish the remaining 50%.
- **September - February:** Multiple rounds of high-speed revision.
- **March:** Final Exams.

By the time Utsav returned in June, he hadn't just missed classes; he had missed half the year's academic load.

Nishant Sir had also created a hierarchy that fueled scarcity and desire:

- **Section A (The Elites):** Strictly 30 students. Best teachers, AC classrooms, English-only environment. Parents fought to pay fees immediately (like Utsav did with his *Dakshina*) to secure a spot before April 2.
- **Section B (The Runners Up):** 60 students. Good, but not elite.
- **Sections C & D:** The crowd and the overflow parking.

Utsav held the "Golden Ticket" to Section A. But sitting at his desk on June 20, surrounded by students who had mastered 50% of the syllabus, he realized the heavy price. A Topper by history, he was now a Backbencher by circumstance. He had to fight both his grief and Nishant Sir's brutal strategy to survive.

The sun over Chronos was unforgiving, but the real heat came from the stifling atmosphere of Class 6-A. It had been nearly three months since the tragic train ride to Radiance.

Sitting in the third row, Utsav stared blankly at Suraj Sir, who was teaching English synonyms. *"To abandon is to leave completely. Synonyms: Forsake, Desert, Renounce."* Utsav felt deserted by time itself.

A sharp knock broke the hum. The peon entered with a circular stamped with the Director's seal. In VIS, a circular was a decree.

Suraj Sir smiled. "The administration has announced the Merit Marathon 2013."

A ripple of electric energy shot through the room. Utsav blinked. The term meant nothing to him.

"This is the ultimate test of retention," Suraj Sir explained. "A compilation of eight hundred questions."

"Four hundred from the Clouds Campus, Sir?" Aditi asked brightly, confirming a fact she already knew.

"Precisely, Aditi. Drafted by the 9th and 10th seniors at the Citadel Branch."

The Citadel Branch commanded reverence; answering their questions was like touching the hem of their robes.

"And the remaining four hundred curated by our faculty here," Suraj Sir added.

"We have exactly one month to memorize them before the OMR sheet test, right Sir?" Muskan chimed in confidently.

"Correct. But remember the condition."

"The Guillotine Rule," Gauri whispered.

"Accurate," Suraj Sir chuckled. "No negative marking. But the test has one hundred questions—eighty from the booklet, twenty fresh application questions. The cut-off is one hundred percent. One mistake, and you are eliminated. We are looking for perfection."

The class gasped with thrill.

"And for the victors?" Qaira leaned forward.

"Their photograph immortalized in the School Album. A gold medal. One month's tuition fee refunded."

"And the School Magazine interview," Aditi added softly.

Utsav sat frozen. Aditi, Muskan, Gauri—they knew the rules and the stakes. They were part of the system. Utsav had no idea what an OMR sheet was. The "Chief Minister" of Class 5 was now just a spectator.

But as the thick booklets landed on his desk with a thud, the fog cleared slightly. He looked at Aditi, already scanning the pages. If he wanted to exist in her world again, he didn't need to catch up on three months of Math. He just needed to memorize eight hundred lines of truth.

The calendar mocked him. Friday, June 28th. The deadline was Sunday. He had to register by tomorrow.

He sat alone during recess, chewing on confusion. A shadow fell across his desk. It was Shyam, his best friend for whom he had skipped Class 2.

"Brother," Shyam tapped the desk. "Are we preparing for this or not?"

"Leave me out of this. You go ahead," Utsav sighed.

"Alone? How can I sit there without you?" Shyam straddled a chair. "Someone from every class will top and be in the School Magazine. Immortal glory."

"What is the point?" Utsav asked flatly.

Shyam smiled mischievously. "What if you and I top?"

"Are you suddenly interested in boys, Shyam?"

"No, you idiot!" Shyam smacked his arm. "Aditi is going to top. That is a universal constant. And Anshu left the school. The competition is open. Just us. We top among the boys, Aditi among the girls."

"What does that achieve?"

"Do you not know Nishant Sir? He is obsessed with symmetry. If two boys and one girl top, where will the photographer place the girl? In the center! You on one side. Me on the other. The perfect frame."

Utsav froze. A permanent record in the archives. Standing beside her—officially and logically.

"Oh..." Utsav whispered.

"If you say 'Oh' one more time, I will chew you alive," Shyam growled playfully.

Reality crashed back. "Dude, my syllabus is barely fifty percent complete. I have backlogs. I cannot afford this distraction."

"But the fee is refunded! Think of the samosas! And you get a medal. Aditi will be impressed."

"You don't understand," Utsav whispered. "You don't know how important it is for me to come Second."

"Why do you settle for Second when you could top the school?" Shyam asked earnestly.

"Seeing her come First feels beautiful. My victory lies in my defeat against her. I want to stand one step behind her, guarding her victory."

Shyam stared in disbelief. "So, this is the game. You are a massive Iceberg. You were coming in Second on purpose!"

"You go ahead, Shyam. I won't do it. This is just the school's theory for making money. Registration is 250 rupees. 660 students. They make over 1.6 lakhs. After refunds, the Director keeps 75,000. This is business."

It was a brilliant, logical argument. But Shyam cared about the mathematics of the heart.

"Brother," Shyam ignored the breakdown. "Aditi will be standing between us. That photograph will make our friendship and our love immortal."

The logic of money and the fear of the syllabus vanished. All Utsav saw was that photo frame.

"Brother. Do you have 250 rupees on you?"

Shyam grinned. "Yes."

"Deposit it. I will pay you back at home."

This was the only motivation Utsav needed.

From that day, Utsav dedicated himself with terrifying focus. Anshu was gone, leaving a vacuum he intended to fill. The Merit Marathon was a rite of passage, training for a ruthless world.

Utsav waited impatiently for July 1st, when the 800 questions would be dictated.

In the back corner of 6-A, a council was in session: Aditi, Muskan, Gauri, Shyam, Utsav, Drishti, and Qaira.

"How will we memorize questions that are out of the syllabus?" Gauri worried.

"They will be memorized. We have a month," Muskan dismissed.

"These people will ask 20 marks worth of questions from anywhere?" Drishti argued.

"Like UPSC exams," Muskan smirked. "The 'area' is decided in the syllabus."

"Nothing is definite," Utsav murmured, calculating. "We will have to work hard for those 20 marks."

"Because the 800 questions are just Halwa (easy pudding)," Muskan laughed.

Utsav smiled—the quiet arrogance of a winner looking at a novice.

"Muskan, I don't think you know who Utsav is," Shyam chuckled.

"The Class 1 Topper. But we are in Class 6 now," she retorted.

"He could top Class 6 easily if he wanted to," Aditi said softly, sketching.

"Hardly," Utsav dropped his voice. "I have been missing for three months. Everything is bouncing over my head. And since when did this GK Book enter the syllabus?"

Aditi stopped drawing. "Three months of holidays. So much enjoyment. You had so much fun cutting loose. Obviously, things will bounce over your head. Studious children don't take such long vacations."

Fun. Enjoyment. Vacation. Utsav smiled, but it didn't reach his eyes. In the echo of her innocent taunt, he heard Chhoti Didi's laugh. He flashed back to the hearse van, the cold train, the pyre.

He could have played the Victim Card. He could have told them he was watching his sister die. They would have offered pity and sympathy.

But Utsav swallowed the truth. A King does not ask for pity. He wanted Aditi's respect, not her sorrow.

"Yeah. Too much fun," he lied smoothly. "By the way, why is the GK book in the syllabus?"

"There is an exam," Aditi replied. "In Class 6, the total paper will be of 900 marks."

"Is it possible the 20 mystery questions will come from this GK book?" Utsav leaned in.

Silence. "Utsav... you are a genius," Gauri whispered.

"We should memorize that book too," Aditi nodded slowly.

"For you people, it is all Halwa," Muskan sighed dramatically. Utsav and Aditi laughed together—the laugh of the elite academic club acknowledging the impossible was just a Tuesday.

"Muskan is craving Halwa way too much," Shyam pointed.

"Halwa was actually made at my house today," Aditi admitted.

"My Mummy makes very tasty Halwa too," Utsav blurted, suddenly shy. "I brought some today. But I felt awkward sharing it."

"Sharing Halwa is a great virtue," Gauri exclaimed.

"Next time, I will share," Utsav smiled.

"In that case, I will bring Salad," Shyam announced proudly.

"Who eats salad with Halwa?" Utsav asked with disgust.

"We need a balanced diet!" Shyam defended.

The back bench erupted in laughter. Nothing was officially finalized, but in that warmth, Utsav felt the first spark of hope. He was back.

Monday arrived with grey, humid July clouds. Utsav arrived early, his bag heavy with empty notebooks. The class geography was set: Zenith Group in the middle, Ojas Enclave Gang in the back, Ether Enclave Traders near the window.

Gupta Sir was teaching when Nishant Sir walked in, handing over papers and pointing out the window.

Peons were dragging carpets onto the grass and testing microphones.

"Are they going to distribute Laddoos?" Shyam whispered loudly.

"No," Aditi analyzed. "That setup is for us. They are going to make us write the questions."

"All 660 of us together?" Utsav corrected her math.

Gupta Sir turned, smiling peculiarly. "270."

The class went silent in shock. "Only 270? But there are over 600 students," Utsav asked.

"How many actually registered?" Gupta Sir noted.

"At least 640 should have," Aditi calculated rapidly. "Otherwise, how will they arrange the funds for prize money and refunds? The math doesn't work."

Gupta Sir sighed, shifting from teacher to mentor. "This is the problem with your generation. You calculate monetary value faster than life values. Vidya International School does not lack funds. We do not need to take money from children to give it back. This is about Merit, not Mathematics."

The class fell silent. The "Business of Education" theory had just been debunked by the teacher they respected most.

The Field of Ink

Ten minutes later, the 270 registered warriors sat cross-legged on the field carpet. Utsav sat next to Shyam, with Aditi and Gauri to their left, and Muskan and Qaira behind them.

The microphone crackled. For the next five hours, from the 1st Period through the 7th, the pen became their shovel and the notebook their trench. The "Council of Class 6-A" kept sanity alive through whispers.

Question: "What is the longest bone in the human body?" "Did he just say 'Fee-mur'?" Muskan whispered. "Sounds like a dying cat." "Shh! Write it before he spells it wrong too," Qaira giggled.

Question: "What is the capital of Turkey?" "Is there a country named Chicken? Why are all countries named after food?" Shyam's stomach rumbled. "Focus, Ojas Enclave. It's Ankara, not Tandoori," Utsav said.

Question: "What is the speed of light?" "Look at her speed," Shyam observed Aditi. "She is writing the answer before the question finishes. Is she a robot?" "No, she is just Aditi. Robots are slower," Utsav replied.

Question: "Spell 'Schizophrenia'." "S... C... H..." the teacher dictated. "He missed the 'I'. It's wrong," Aditi whispered. "Should we correct him?" Gauri asked. "No. Let others get it wrong. Less competition." Aditi winked.

At 1:30 PM, the marathon ended. Legs numb, fingers stained, 270 students walked to the gate like returning soldiers.

"Why make us work so hard?" Utsav flexed his cramped fingers. "They could have given us a printout. We paid."

"Sahabzaade wants the whole school to serve him for 250 Rupees," Muskan scoffed.

"The Prince of Ojas Enclave has arrived," Utsav grinned as Shyam appeared. "I am nothing before the King of West Albizia," Shyam bowed.

Aditi laughed. "You boys just play 'Respect-Respect' all day."

"Does Memsaab Muskan also want respect?" Gauri asked. "Yes! When rich people are called rich, they get excited," Muskan retorted. "Why are you so jealous, Muskan?" Gauri asked. "It isn't our fault we are wealthy." "Rich people sit on the rights of the poor," Muskan channeled her inner revolutionary.

Utsav smirked. "Muskan. Your family owns a Dairy? You have a Scooty? Your house is three stories high? How exactly are you poor?"

Caught, Muskan stammered, "I can't even imagine what you people have hidden away!" "So, you are from the Income Tax Department?" Gauri clapped.

Shyam wrapped an arm around Utsav. "You eventually become the very thing you hate, Muskan. Be careful, you might end up rich."

By the lunch bell, they had only reached Question 400. "My fingers are numb. Is this a stenography center?" Shyam dropped his pen. "It's the filter," Utsav whispered, massaging his wrist and glancing at Aditi. "The weak stop writing. The winners ask for a new refill."

During lunch, the Council gathered. "Still think it's Halwa?" Gauri looked exhausted. "Half Halwa," Muskan chewed slowly. "400 down. Then the mystery 20 marks."

Aditi turned around. "The Citadel questions were tough. Question 312? Higgs Boson? That is 10th-grade Physics."

"By rote," Utsav said calmly. "We just need to know Higgs Boson equals God Particle. It's a memory game, not an IQ test."

Aditi looked at him. The "Class 5 Utsav"—the genius—flashed in her eyes. "You seem very confident for someone who missed three months."

"I might have missed the syllabus, but I haven't lost my memory. I will eat them up."

"Like Halwa?" Shyam grinned. "Like Halwa," Utsav affirmed.

The second day was grueling. The sun baked the grounds. Aditi led her group to the shade of a massive Neem tree.

Question: "What is the process by which plants make their own food?" "I wish I had chlorophyll," Shyam sighed. "I could stand in the sun and get lunch." "You aren't turning green, Shyam. You are turning roasted," Utsav noted.

Question: "Which city is the City of Joy?" "Write 'Vidya International School'," Shyam said. "Watching Utsav write fast gives me joy." "Write 'Ojas Enclave'. The jokers live there," Utsav replied.

Question: "How many players in a Cricket team?" "11 players and 1 Shyam who just looks at the girls' stand," Utsav answered. "That is fielding, brother. Deep observation," Shyam countered.

Question: "What is the National Motto of India?" "Satyameva Jayate," Aditi said. "Lie. The motto should be 'Exam Alone Triumphs'," Shyam groaned. "Truth triumphs, Shyam. That is why Aditi is Rank 1 and you are... happy," Utsav smiled.

The dictation ended. Transitioning from blinding sunlight to the dim classroom was brutal.

"I have gone blind!" Shyam stumbled in the dark. "Blind is fine, but leave my hair!" Gauri screamed. "Shyam has my hair!" Aditi yelled. "Then who has my hair?" Muskan shouted.

Gauri swiped her nails in the dark. "Ouch!" Utsav yelped. "I didn't know it was your hair!" "Sorry!" Shyam finally released his grip.

Retinas adjusted. The group collapsed onto the back benches for the 7th period.

"They should have dictated 400 more," Aditi complained. "And told us the 20 marks would come from those." "So what? It's the same ratio," Shyam shrugged. "Probability doesn't work like that," Muskan pitied him.

"What were you guys doing pulling hair?" Zaid interrupted. "It's the pupil," Zaid explained the science of light adjustment. "The Ether Enclave people know things other than Business?" Utsav smirked.

"At least we don't conduct Pooja for a living," Rajat sneered, taking a direct hit at Utsav’s priesthood work.

"People who get girls on the strength of their Massi shouldn't think so loud," Shyam stepped in.

Utsav stopped Shyam and turned to Rajat with King-like eyes. "Son. Your exam copies are lighter than the amount of 'lightly' you take me."

Rajat backed down. "Whatever. Just stay away from my Massi."

"Oh. So that is the matter," Utsav exhaled. He plucked a Neem twig, stripped the leaves, and handed it to Muskan. "Muskan, from today, you are my sister." He turned to Rajat. "You need proof of dignity. Here it is."

A piece of the twig landed on Aditi’s bag.

"I also want to make someone my brother. Any offers?" Aditi smiled mischievously.

Utsav instantly thrust Shyam’s hand forward. "Here!" "No!" Shyam yelped, snatching his hand back.

Both boys sprinted out of the class. Utsav returned carrying Aditi’s little brother, Rachit. "Tie the Rakhi to him. He is the original. Leave us duplicates alone."

Aditi burst into laughter. The tension broke. Utsav pulled Rajat into a group hug.

"We are rich people," Shyam clapped Rajat. "We need to live in unity so everyone else burns watching us."

Utsav hugged Muskan tighter, remembering when she had slapped him in Class 4 for getting chalk dust on her suit. "Muskan. If chalk falls on you from now on... explain it with love. Don't hit me."

Guilt washed over her as she remembered his hidden tears. "I'm sorry," she started. "It's okay, sister," he patted her head.

July 19th. The monsoon cast grey light into 6-A. It was Ayushi's birthday, meaning free chocolate.

Vice Principal Sir walked in. "Faculty meeting. Four free periods. Memorize quietly."

Silence evaporated instantly. The gang rearranged on the back benches. Eight people. Infinite topics.

"Tejas probably eats the entire Ether Enclave," Shyam eyed the chocolates. "That is why Rajat's weight isn't increasing," Muskan smirked. "You shouldn't body-shame," Aditi said sternly. "You are so perfect, you already make the world feel inferior," Utsav shot back. "You don't need to shame anyone; your existence is enough."

"I am sensing something here," Shyam whistled as Utsav's ears turned red.

"Brother, how old have you become?" Rajat asked Utsav. "I will be 9 tomorrow." "Tomorrow is your Birthday?" Aditi asked. "No," Shyam interrupted. "Utsav creates his own age."

"What do you want to become?" Rajat asked. "Utsav wants to become Prime Minister," Shyam said. "With full attitude." "I'll do CA," Utsav laughed. "What is Commerce?" Gauri asked. "In 9th grade, we have an option: Commerce, Arts, or Science," Aditi explained.

"What is all this?" Shyam panicked. "We decided we would become Doctors." "Homeopathy," Utsav nodded. "The sweet pill doctor."

The countdown began. The Marathon was a lifestyle.

At the water cooler, Shyam noted, "The mirror image reverses left and right but not up and down." "That is Physics," Utsav said. "Focus on the 800. Who invented the flush toilet?"

During lunch, Aditi traded Poha for answers. "I'll give two spoons for Question 672." "Formic Acid," Muskan ate Maggi. "This is a black market of knowledge."

At 9:30 PM, Utsav got a call on his Nokia C101. "Utsav, quick. Question 780. The train speed," Aditi demanded. "Relative speed 10 km/h. They meet in 2 hours," Utsav whispered. "Goodnight... Topper."

"My brain feels like a squeezed sponge," Utsav said in assembly. "Just 5 more days," Aditi encouraged.

Gupta Sir drew an OMR sheet. "Darken the circle completely. If you go outside, the machine rejects it." "What if my hand shakes?" Shyam sweat. "Then your career shakes."

At the Shiv Temple, Utsav prayed. "Asking for Question 14 to be 'Capital of India'."

The heavens opened on Exam Day. Students arrived splashing through knee-deep water.

Utsav met a pale Shyam. "My brain is leaking." "It's waterproof. Just don't shake your head," Utsav gripped his shoulder.

Nishant Sir announced: "100 Questions. 120 Minutes. One mistake, you are out."

The first 80 were speed. Utsav didn't read; he recognized sentence shapes. He wasn't answering; he was building a photo frame with Aditi. Aditi was an artist, carefully spiraling bubbles. Shyam smiled, remembering moments with friends that tied to answers.

Then came the "Mystery 20".

Question 85: Average speed of 60kmph and 40kmph. Utsav remembered Gupta Sir's lecture. *2xy / (x+y).* He calculated 48.

Bubble B. Shyam struggled, then remembered Utsav's trick. Harmonic Mean. 48. *Thank you, Utsav.*

Question 92: NOT a constitutional right. Aditi remembered her father talking about property disputes. Right to Property. Bubble C.

Question 100: Father of Abhimanyu? Arjuna. A gift. But a sweat drop fell on Shyam's OMR sheet between C and D. He dabbed it like a surgeon and engraved Bubble C over the damp spot.

"Pens Down!"

The exam was over. Shyam had fought a war with sweat, but scored 100. Aditi had navigated the tricky speed question. They walked to the canteen—Utsav, Aditi, Shyam—exactly the photograph Utsav dreamed of.

In the Staff Room, Badi Didi checked Aditi's sheet. 100/100. She asked Deeksha Ma'am about Utsav. "Brilliant," Deeksha Ma'am sighed. "But he missed Question 92. 99 out of 100." Badi Didi hid her disappointment. In the Marathon, 99 was zero.

The ten days waiting for results were torture. Utsav was pale. "I marked 'Right to Education'." "You marked 'Right to Property'. Trust your muscle memory," Zaid assured.

Utsav and Aditi sat silently. He slid a note: *Whatever happens, we tried.* She wrote back: *We didn't just try. We conquered.*

The rain drowned Chronos. It was a "Rainy Day Exception" with no uniforms required. Utsav, however, wore his school uniform.

Navigating the slippery slush, he reached the taps. The Zenith Trio approached. Gauri slipped, swinging her arm, nudging Utsav. He lost his footing, dropping to one muddy knee. His pristine uniform was ruined.

"I am so sorry!" Gauri gasped. "It's okay," Utsav burned with embarrassment, feeling small among the casual clothes.

He tried to wash it, but the mud was stubborn. Aditi stepped closer in her red floral suit. She knelt.

"Aditi? What are you doing?"

She cupped water and gently splashed his knee, using her clean, fair hands to rub the mud off his trousers.

The corridor went silent. Boys watched in disbelief. "Queen behavior," Shyam whispered.

Utsav was paralyzed by a crushing sense of shame. The roles were reversed. He felt weak.

"Aditi, stop. Everyone is looking."

Aditi washed her hands, eyes devoid of pity. "It's done. Be careful next time."

Utsav stood there. The memory was searing into his soul. Years later, he would forget the marks, but he would never forget the water on his knee and the girl who didn't mind getting her hands dirty for him.

Monsoon of Unspoken Melodies

August 2013. The monsoon had completely swallowed the city of Chronos. The skies over Vidya International School were a permanent, bruised grey, unleashing torrential downpours that turned the pristine campus into a chaotic mosaic of puddles and mud. For the students of Class 6-A, the heavy rain was a thrilling excuse for chaos, canceled sports periods, and humid classroom gossip.

But for Utsav, the monsoon was simply another season of silent, invisible sacrifices. His love for Aditi was exactly like the Chronos rain—constant, overwhelming, and entirely out of his control.

The morning began with a sudden, violent deluge just as the school buses and rickshaws arrived at the main gate. Aditi stepped out of her transport, clutching her school bag to her chest. She had forgotten her umbrella. She stood stranded under the tiny canvas roof of the rickshaw, looking helplessly at the fifty-meter open walkway leading to the safe, dry porch of the school building.

Utsav was walking a few paces behind her. In his hand, he held a large, sturdy black umbrella.

He wanted nothing more than to walk up to her, open it over her head, and walk her to the class. But he knew the rules of the schoolyard. Approaching her directly would draw unwanted attention, spark endless teasing from the boys, and worst of all, it might make her uncomfortable. His love was a secret he guarded with his life.

Just then, Rajat stepped out of his father's sleek sedan. He was wearing an expensive, imported waterproof jacket. Rajat glanced at Aditi, but instead of offering to shield her, he pulled his hood up to protect his gel-spiked hair and sprinted toward the building, terrified of ruining his polished shoes.

Utsav's jaw tightened. He didn't hesitate. He walked briskly to the school watchman standing near the gate. Slipping a ten-rupee note from his pocket into the guard's hand, he handed over his black umbrella.

"Uncle," Utsav whispered urgently. "Go to that girl in the braids. Tell her you found this in the lost-and-found yesterday and it belongs to the school. Tell her to use it."

Before the guard could argue, Utsav pulled his heavy school bag over his head and sprinted directly into the merciless downpour. The cold, heavy rain soaked him instantly. Icy water seeped through his white shirt and grey trousers, chilling him to the bone. But as he reached the porch and shook the water from his hair, he turned back.

He saw the watchman handing the large black umbrella to Aditi. She opened it, a radiant sigh of relief washing over her beautiful face, and walked safely to the building, completely dry.

Utsav stood shivering in the cold corridor, his lips turning slightly blue, but a warm, invincible smile spread across his face. *She is safe from the storm. That is all that matters.*

When Utsav entered Class 6-A, the room was a zoo of humidity and wet uniforms.

Shyam was leaning out the window, vigorously wringing out his wet socks. "Brother, look at you!" Shyam gasped. "Did you swim to school today?"

"I just like the rain," Utsav lied smoothly, his teeth chattering.

Tejas pushed his fogged-up glasses up his nose, holding a textbook like a shield. "Actually, getting soaked in this specific cumulonimbus downpour increases your chances of hypothermia by forty percent."

"Tejas, please keep your meteorological depression to yourself," Gauri snapped from the second row. She and Ayushi were frantically trying to fix their frizzy hair, using the reflection of a shiny steel geometry box.

"I brought extra aloo parathas because of the weather!" Ayushi announced, instantly changing the mood of the room.

Qaira and Drishti immediately abandoned their bags and crowded around Ayushi's desk. "You are an absolute angel, Ayushi! The canteen pakoras are going to be soggy today anyway," Qaira cheered.

On the other side of the room, sheer chaos reigned. Vikram, the resident menace of the backbenches, was intentionally shaking his wet head like a golden retriever, spraying water all over Chinmay's open notebook.

"Are you crazy, Vikram?!" Chinmay yelled, aggressively shoving him back. "The ink is bleeding! My homework is ruined!"

Nearby, Sneha, Sakshi, and Kashish had formed a highly defensive human shield around their group project file. "If one single drop of water touches this chart paper, I will personally throw whoever did it out the window," Sakshi warned, her eyes darting fiercely between Vikram and Chinmay's scuffle.

Near the back of the room, Niharika and Zoha were groaning, engaged in a tug-of-war with a jammed glass window that was letting a steady mist of rain blow onto their seats. "It's completely stuck! The wood is swollen from the moisture," Zoha complained, pulling at the latch while Niharika tried to push the heavy glass shut.

Through all this noise and damp chaos, Aditi walked in.

She looked immaculate. Not a single drop of rain had touched her. Her twin braids were perfect, her uniform crisp and dry. She smiled at Muskan, completely unaware of the boy in the third row who was currently freezing so she could look this flawless.

As Aditi walked toward her seat in the front row, Utsav noticed something chilling. The ceiling right above Aditi's wooden desk had a minor leak. A slow, steady drip of dirty rainwater was pooling right on the wooden bench where she was about to sit.

Aditi was busy looking the other way, laughing at a joke Muskan had just told.

Utsav didn't think twice. He stood up, grabbed a dry cloth duster from the blackboard ledge, and walked over. In one swift, silent motion, he wiped her seat completely dry. But the ceiling was still dripping.

Acting perfectly natural, Utsav casually bumped his hip against the heavy wooden desk, shifting the entire desk-and-bench unit three inches to the left. The dirty water drop from the ceiling now fell harmlessly onto the aisle floor. He walked back to his seat just as Aditi turned around and sat down comfortably.

"Why are you rearranging the furniture, Utsav?" Muskan narrowed her eyes at him suspiciously.

"Just stretching my legs, Muskan," Utsav replied softly, sitting back down in his damp, uncomfortable clothes.

By the third period, the high humidity in the air began to wreak havoc on the students' stationery. Gupta Sir was writing complex Math fractions on the blackboard at lightning speed.

Aditi was writing furiously when her pen suddenly stopped. She shook it. She scribbled aggressively on the back page of her notebook. Nothing. The moisture had jammed the rollerball.

"Muskan, do you have a spare blue pen?" Aditi whispered frantically.

"Only a red one," Muskan whispered back, not looking up from her notes.

Aditi turned slightly to the row behind her. "Rajat? Do you have a spare pen?"

Rajat looked down at his imported Pierre Cardin pen. "Sorry Aditi, I only brought this one. It's very delicate, you know? The ink is from France. I can't risk breaking it."

Aditi bit her lip in genuine panic. Gupta Sir was already picking up the duster to erase the board.

Utsav was watching everything from his desk. He only had two pens in his bag. One was a cheap, scratchy ballpoint that tore the paper if pressed too hard, and the other was a brand-new, smooth-flowing Reynolds Trimax—his prized possession, reserved only for writing exams.

He uncapped the Trimax, checked that it wrote perfectly on his own hand, and then purposely dropped it onto the floor. With the side of his wet shoe, he gently and precisely kicked it forward. It rolled smoothly under the desks and stopped exactly near Aditi's left shoe.

Aditi looked down. "Oh! A pen!" She picked it up, looking around the room. "Whose is this?"

Utsav kept his head buried deep in his notebook, aggressively scratching notes with his terrible, skipping ballpoint pen, acting completely absorbed in the math problem.

"Must be someone from the previous period," Rajat said dismissively. "Just use it, Aditi, he's erasing the board."

Aditi un-capped Utsav's pen. It glided over her notebook like butter. She sighed in deep relief, copying the complex equations perfectly before the board was wiped clean. Utsav's handwriting for the rest of the day looked like a spider had crawled through an inkpot and danced on his pages, but he didn't care at all. His pen was in her hand. For him, that was the ultimate privilege.

When the final bell rang at 2:00 PM, the rain had stopped, but the school courtyard had transformed into a minefield of deep, muddy puddles.

The crowd of Class 6-A moved toward the main gate. Aditi was walking ahead with Gauri and Niharika, chatting about the homework. Utsav was walking a few paces behind them with Shyam and Tejas.

Ahead of them, a massive, unavoidable puddle spanned the width of the walkway. Suddenly, a group of rowdy senior boys came running blindly toward the gate, their heavy shoes splashing muddy water everywhere.

Rajat, who had been walking near Aditi, immediately sidesteps in panic. "Watch out, my trousers will get stained!" he complained loudly, jumping to the dry edge of the path and leaving Aditi completely exposed to the incoming splash zone.

Utsav's protective instincts flared. He sped up his pace, seamlessly overtaking Aditi just as the seniors ran past. The heavy splash of muddy water flew through the air, aimed directly at Aditi's crisp white uniform.

But it hit Utsav instead.

He took the entire splash on his left leg and side, acting as a human shield. The thick brown mud splattered across his already damp trousers and shirt. Aditi gasped, taking a step back. She remained perfectly, flawlessly clean.

"Oh my god, Utsav!" Gauri exclaimed, her eyes wide. "Those seniors are entirely blind! Look at your uniform!"

Utsav looked down at the dark brown mud ruining his white shirt. He casually brushed it off, though it only smeared the dirt deeper into the fabric.

"It's fine, Gauri. Just a little dirt," Utsav said calmly. He didn't look at Aditi for credit. He didn't say, *I did this for you.* He simply accepted the mess because it belonged to him now, not her.

Aditi looked at his mud-soaked uniform, then at the pristine, clean hem of her own skirt. A soft, slightly puzzled expression crossed her face. "You should be more careful, Utsav," she said gently, her voice full of sweet concern.

"I will be," he replied, his eyes impossibly warm. *As long as you are safe, I don't mind the mud.*

As the crowd dispersed outside the gates, Shyam walked beside Utsav toward their respective transports.

"You are a complete and utter idiot, do you know that?" Shyam muttered, shaking his head in disbelief. "I saw you give the guard your umbrella this morning. You ruined your own clothes twice today. You gave up your good pen. And she doesn't even know you did any of it."

Utsav smiled, looking up at the bruised grey sky of Chronos. The cool monsoon wind hit his wet, muddy clothes, making him shiver violently, but his heart felt like a roaring hearth fire.

"Shyam, true love isn't a transaction," Utsav whispered, his voice barely audible over the chaotic sound of the traffic on the Chronicle-Nectar Highway. "It doesn't require an audience. It doesn't need an invoice, and it certainly doesn't demand gratitude. Knowing she is smiling, knowing she is dry, knowing her notes are complete... that is my return on investment."

He walked toward his bus, shivering, stained, and completely exhausted. To the rest of the world, Utsav was just a clumsy boy who forgot his umbrella and slipped in the mud.

But in the quiet, sacred sanctuary of his own mind, he was the King of the Monsoon, proudly standing guard over the only Queen that mattered.

August 10, 2013

The wait was over. Arjun Sir walked in with a sheet of paper.

"The Management is very strict this year. Only those with 100% accuracy have been selected. From Class 6-A, we have three students who achieved the impossible."

Shyam squeezed his eyes shut. Utsav gripped his desk, expecting the heartbreak of '99'.

"First, Aditi." The class erupted. Aditi smiled composedly.

"Second, Ayushi." Ayushi gasped, dropping her pencil.

"And third," Arjun Sir looked directly at Utsav. "Utsav."

Shyam screamed, jumping on Utsav, shaking the bench. Utsav sat stunned. *100? But Badi Didi looked so worried...* He looked toward the Staff Room door. Badi Didi leaned against the frame, shocked but slowly breaking into a proud smile. Deeksha Ma'am must have maintained secrecy for the surprise element.

Principal Sir entered with a silver tray bearing three envelopes and three gold medals. He handed Aditi her cash refund envelope. Ayushi grinned widely. Utsav took his light envelope, feeling the immense weight of the cold medal around his neck.

Shyam clapped the loudest, cheering for his best friend. Utsav touched the medal. He had done it. He was immortal.

The Frame of Symmetry August 11, 2013. The School Garden.

"Wear your best uniforms," they were told for the School Journal photoshoot.

Nishant Sir, a man of aesthetics, directed the photographer. "We have two girls and one boy. Symmetry dictates the boy must be in the center."

Utsav's heart skipped a beat.

"Utsav, middle. Aditi, left. Ayushi, right."

Utsav stepped into position. To his right, Ayushi beamed. To his left, Aditi looked beautiful, her gold medal glinting.

Utsav looked at the lens, realizing the irony. He had dreamed of a photo with Shyam and Aditi. Instead, Shyam was behind the camera making funny faces, and Utsav was forever framed as the genius of Class 6-A.

"Smile!" *Click.*

The glory faded quickly. The gold medal hung in West Albizia, but at school, The Backlog awaited.

Utsav had missed April, May, and June. While 6-A revised, he was learning for the first time. His schedule became a blur of ink and exhaustion:

- **02:00 PM:** Lunch eaten while writing.
- **03:00 PM:** Copy from Aditi's perfect Science notebook.
- **05:00 PM:** Decipher Shyam's nightmare Maths notebook.
- **07:00 PM:** Tuition with Gupta Sir. Here, he wasn't the "Merit Marathon Winner"; he was the boy who didn't know integers.
- **11:00 PM:** Memorize Sanskrit shlokas until his eyes burned.

He was the "Iceberg," looking calm but paddling against a tsunami.

Vidya International School's strategy for Half-Yearly Exams was "Academic Drilling."

- **Maths Drill:** Gupta Sir fired shots. "Question 4! Logic only. Rajat, stand up! LCM?" "Wrong. HCF. Minus 5 marks."
- **Science Sprint:** Sundeep Sir demanded precision. "Write 'Loss of water in the form of vapor', or I deduct half a mark."
- **History Rapid Fire:** Abhimanyu Sir turned history into a buzzer round. "Harappa?" "1921!"

Ojas Enclave was known for rowdy boys. The "Backbench Lords" were led by Vikram—tall, broad, and mean-spirited.

"Oye, Joker," Vikram sneered, kicking Shyam's bench during tiffin. "Got 50 marks? Are you half a man too? Show us the monkey dance."

Shyam looked down. "Leave it, Vikram."

"Who gave you permission to speak?" Vikram raised a hand to slap him.

A smaller hand intercepted it. Utsav. "Don't touch him. He is not your toy."

Vikram laughed. "What will you do, dwarf?" He grabbed the back of Utsav's neck, squeezing hard and violently jerking his head down and sideways.

Crack. A blinding sprain shot through Utsav's neck. He gasped, head locked in a tilted position.

"That's for interfering," Vikram spat.

"Vikram!" Aditi cut through the corridor. The "Rank 1" aura froze the bullies. "Get lost. Before I call Head Sir."

Vikram walked away. Aditi rushed to Utsav. "Are you okay? Look up."

"I can't. It hurts." Utsav gritted his teeth.

Aditi stepped closer. Utsav hadn't hit his growth spurt; his head reached her chest. "Hold still." She placed her cool right hand on his throbbing neck.

A jolt went through Utsav's body. It felt like soothing ointment. "Is it hurting here?" she asked softly, massaging the muscle.

10 seconds. That's all it took. The sharp pain simply evaporated. The sprain vanished.

Utsav wanted to look up and smile, but his strategic brain kicked in. If he showed Zaid, Rajat, and Vikram's gang that her touch cured him instantly, they would mock him mercilessly, or worse, break his neck for real.

The pain was gone, but the acting had to continue.

"Is it better?" she pulled her hand away.

Utsav kept his head stiffly tilted. "A little. But it's still locked. I'll manage. Just... don't touch it. It hurts," he lied to protect the sanctity of the moment.

For History and English, Utsav sat like a stiff statue. He walked to the bus like a robot, reveling in Aditi's guilty, concerned glances. *She cares.*

Back in his room, he rolled his neck freely. Zero pain. He flopped onto his bed, smiling. The injury was real, but the cure was a secret. The sensation of her cooling touch was engraved in his heart forever.

The next day, pressure led to comparisons of "Study Environments."

"I fall asleep under my cold AC," Gauri complained. "My cooler makes so much noise I memorize answers to the beat," Muskan rolled her eyes. "I use the 'All-in-One' Guide and eat biryani in my dad's AC office," Zaid laughed. "My Massi bought me a lamp," Rajat said. "Now I sleep with a spotlight on my face." "In Ojas Enclave, electricity goes out constantly. I study by candlelight like Lincoln," Shyam sighed. "He lights the candle, makes a wax ball, and goes to sleep," Utsav corrected him. The group laughed, breaking the tension.

The syllabus was completed. Free periods turned 6-A into a parliament of strategy.

"Focus on Chapter 5," Aditi dictated from the center. "Are you sure? It's dry," Zaid chewed his nails. "If Aditi says it, it is law," Utsav stated. "Has anyone seen the seating arrangement?" Gauri asked. "Alphabetical," Muskan said. "I am U. Near the door. Good for fresh air," Utsav calculated. "I am A. Front row. Can't even stretch," Aditi sighed.

The Final Exams arrived. The school was in chaos.

"What is the formula for Perimeter of a Rectangle?" Ayushi panicked. "2 into (L plus B)," the group chanted.

Utsav looked at Aditi muttering dates. "You will top again." "And you?" Aditi asked. "I ran a marathon to catch up. I won't beat you, but I won't be far behind."

"Vice Principal Sir is on duty for Maths!" Shyam squeezed in. "RIP to my slip-system."

The Half-Yearly War began. Vice Principal Sir patrolled like a shark. Stuck on Question 4, Shyam caught an eraser Zaid threw. Microscopic ink read: *Solid to Gas*. Shyam smiled.

Vice Principal Sir stopped. "Nice eraser, Shyam. Keep the knowledge in your brain next time." He pocketed it. Shyam spent the rest of the exam erasing with his thumb.

In History, Muskan raised her hand. "The map is too small. Sri Lanka is falling off the desk." "Just fold the ocean, genius," Gauri whispered.

In Hindi, Ayushi hummed a poem to remember lines. "Are you singing for a reality show?" Arjun Sir asked. "No Sir. Just feeling the emotion of the flower." "Sir, she is the flower. We are the thorns," Rajat quipped. "Rajat, 5 marks deducted for bad poetry."

In Maths, Utsav asked for a Supplementary Sheet after 45 minutes. The class looked up. *Are you writing a novel?* Shyam watched in horror. Two minutes later, Aditi asked for one too. The competition was silent, but deadly.

Exams ended. Students were in a strange limbo.

Utsav and Zaid "accidentally" walked past the Staff Room. "I see a red circle. Zero or hundred?" Zaid asked. "It's a coffee stain. Stop analyzing stains," Utsav said. "Admire the architecture from your classroom," Gupta Sir caught them. "Or I will admire your parents' reaction to your marks."

"I missed a step in Pythagoras," Aditi worried. "You wrote three pages for a 5-mark question. You invented new steps," Gauri sighed.

"If we pray, maybe the Maths papers will get lost," Shyam gathered the group. "I am praying for Aditi to get one mark less than me," Ayushi said. "I heard that!" Aditi walked by.

Result Day.

Gupta Sir entered 6-A holding a long, scrolled list: The "Death Warrant." The class went pin-drop silent.

"The results this year are... interesting," he began, reading the marks out of 900.

"Preeti... 570." A gasp. The silent topper from Panchvati had crashed. "Aditi... 864." The class erupted. 96%. Aditi smiled modestly, relieved. She was still Queen.

"Utsav... 810." Utsav slumped back. 90%. Despite missing three months, he had crossed the barrier. He was safe.

"Ayushi... 806." Ayushi groaned. "Just four marks behind Utsav!" "Better luck next time, Birthday Girl," Utsav grinned.

"Gauri... 830." Gauri high-fived Muskan. She had beaten Utsav.

"Shyam... 450." "Yes!" Shyam pumped his fist. "Exact 50%! Half-Yearly, Half-Marks! Perfectly balanced!" The tension broke with laughter.

Utsav looked at the top 3 on the board:

1. Aditi (864)
2. Gauri (830)
3. Utsav (810)

He was Rank 3. Aditi caught his eye and gave a small thumbs-up. Utsav smiled back, but inside, a fire burned. *Next time, there will be no gap. The photo frame will be perfect.*

The class buzzed. Aditi broke away from her congratulatory swarm and walked to Utsav.

"Congratulations, Rank 3," Aditi said softly, offering her hand.

Utsav shook it. "Congratulations, Rank 1. The gap is big this time. 54 marks."

"You missed three months, Utsav," Aditi reminded him. "To get 90%... it is incredible. You should be happy."

"I am happy," Utsav lied smoothly.

Aditi tilted her head. "Your mouth is laughing. But your eyes... they are calculating. You are already planning the Annual Exams."

Utsav's smile dropped for a fraction of a second. "Next time, there will be no backlog. And that gap of 54 marks? I will burn it down."

"I'll be waiting," Aditi smiled. "The view from the top is lonely. I need competition."

Utsav went to the washroom, splashing cold water on his face. He looked in the mirror. "Third," he whispered, clenching his fist. "Never again. Aditi is fine. But Gauri? No one else stands between us."

The backbench hierarchy shifted. Gauri walked with a new swagger.

"It is so hot today," Gauri fanned herself. "Maybe because I am glowing from my marks. 830."

"Enjoy it while it lasts," Muskan rolled her eyes. "Next time, the sleeping giant will wake up."

"I got 450," Shyam stood on the desk rail. "The probability of getting exactly half is rarer than getting 100%. I am the chosen one."

"You are the 'Just Passed' one. Sit down before you fall," Aditi said.

"West Albizia lost to M. Block," Gauri smirked at Utsav. "How does it feel to lose to the 'Rich Girl'?"

Utsav smiled a lazy, dangerous smile. "It feels... refreshing. Chivalry isn't dead. I opened the door for you."

"Utsav, admit it. She studied harder," Aditi laughed.

"She did," Utsav nodded at Gauri. "But remember. The Half-Yearly is a rehearsal. The Annual is the premiere. Don't get too comfortable."

"Knowledge is power," Aditi said firmly. "Money can disappear. But what is in Utsav's head... no one can steal that."

"Someone can steal his heart though," Shyam whispered loudly to Rajat.

"My aim with a chalk is still 100%, Shyam," Utsav warned.

"Rank 3 is the best! Long live West Albizia!" Shyam yelled.

The school accelerated. Final Exams loomed. Late at night, studying alone under his lamp, Utsav missed his friends. The voices of the backbenchers had become the background music of his life.

Kuldeep Sir erased the board furiously. Time was short for the Hindi syllabus. "We finished reading. I will give a quick crash course summary of April and May stories."

"Sir, this is cheating," Shyam raised his hand. "In April, you acted out the characters. Now it feels like a news report."

"Where is the time?" Aditi sighed. "We have to study strategically."

"At least you guys saw the movie," Utsav muttered. "I wasn't in Chronos. This news report is all I have."

"The stories are for entertainment," Kuldeep Sir said. "The real challenge is Grammar. Sandhi, Samas, Alankar. Nominate yourselves for mandatory Extra Classes at 7:00 AM sharp."

October 22, 2013. 7:30 AM.

Winter fog settled over Chronos. The "Nominated Bunch" sat in the cold classroom. Kuldeep Sir was explaining word joining.

Shyam walked in, dragging his helmet, yawning wildly. "Sir. Why is there so much struggle in life? You've been waiting 30 minutes for me."

"We were not waiting for you, Shyam," Kuldeep Sir said dryly. "Park your cycle and sit. When two sounds meet to form a new word, it is Sandhi. Example: Vidya + Aalaya = Vidyalaya."

"Just like... Utsav + Aditi = Adyotsav," Gauri whispered behind Utsav.

Utsav choked. Aditi turned bright red. "That's not even grammatically correct!" Utsav whispered, scandalized.

"It sounds nice though," Gauri giggled. "The Divine Festival."

After Assembly, Principal Sir walked into 6-A, his leather shoes clicking ominously. He looked deeply disappointed.

"Ever since Section A and B merged, discipline is zero. You think you are Class 6 seniors? Let's see if you know the basics." He pointed to a boy. "Spell Sunday."

"S-U-N-D-A-Y."

"Sit. You. Spell Tuesday."

"T-U-E-S-D-A-Y."

"Sit. You. Spell Wednesday."

"W-E-N-S-D-A-Y?"

"Wrong! Stand! You?"

"W-E-D-N-S-D-A-Y?"

"Wrong! Stand!"

The class rose like dominoes. The tricky 'E' trapped everyone. Soon, only Aditi and Utsav remained seated.

Principal Sir looked at the two sitting islands. Aditi and Utsav exchanged a shared smile—the secret language of the intelligent. *We are safe.*

"Aditi, Utsav. Stand up." The Principal ordered. "Test of coordination. Spell it together. Alternating letters. Go."

Aditi: "W" Utsav: "E" Aditi: "D" Utsav: "N" Aditi: "E" Utsav: "S"

Ping-Pong. Fast and sharp. Then came the second 'D'.

Aditi: "D"

Utsav opened his mouth for 'A', but made the mistake of looking at her. Her eyes were bright, a stray lock of hair fell over her forehead, her lips shaping the letter 'D'.

The spelling vanished from Utsav's mind. He stared at the girl who made intelligence look like magic.

"D..." Aditi whispered urgently, tilting her head.

The Principal raised an eyebrow. "Utsav?"

The trance broke. "A!" Utsav blurted. "Y," Aditi finished.

"Good. Sit down," the Principal nodded.

Aditi sighed in relief. "You got stuck? I thought you forgot."

"No," Utsav lied, ears burning. "I just choked."

To the class, it was a lucky escape. To Utsav, it was a permanent bookmark. He didn't care about the spelling; he only cared about that middle moment where time stopped, and the smartest girl in class looked only at him, waiting for his voice.

Days later, Vice Principal Sir entered with an older man. "My brother, Mr. Pandey, a retired professor, will take your class today. Show respect."

Mr. Pandey scanned the room like a hawk. "Shyam. Stand up. In which Continent does India fall?"

Shyam scratched his head. "Continent... sunke mujhe Continental Food ki yaad aa gayi. I am feeling hungry, Sir."

The class giggled.

"Sit down. Useless. Rajat. Same question."

Rajat froze under the pressure. "Africa? No... Europe?"

"Sit down! Zero General Knowledge. Only fashion." His eyes landed on the second row. "The girl with the braid. Stand up."

Aditi stood with perfect posture. "Sir, India is in the Asia continent. Specifically, South Asia."

Mr. Pandey smiled a cracked smile. "Excellent! This girl... she is the future. She is the Gold Medallist."

After he left, the classroom turned into a debate ground.

"Wasn't that too much?" Utsav complained. "Everyone knows Asia. For one word, he predicted her whole future? Unfair."

"Unfair?" Gauri defended Aditi. "He asked Shyam and Rajat first. They blew it. Aditi picked up the gold coin they dropped."

"I would have answered if I wasn't focused on my stomach," Shyam sighed.

Aditi turned to face Utsav analytically. "It's not about one word. It's about the sample. Think of a pressure cooker. To check if rice is cooked, we press two grains. If they are cooked, we assume the whole pot is. He checked three grains. Shyam was raw. Rajat was raw. I was cooked. He assumed the quality based on the sample."

Brilliant, logical explanation. But Utsav argued, "We are not clones like rice grains! We are different humans!"

"Correct, Utsav," Gauri smirked. "But if you put Basmati, Brown Rice, and Khichdi Rice in the same cooker, you check them individually because they cook at different speeds." She pointed at Shyam and Rajat. "Clearly, some grains in this class are never going to get cooked."

Utsav watched silently. *She thinks she is just a grain of rice. She doesn't realize she is the Saffron in a pot of plain white rice. You don't check Saffron; you just smell the fragrance.*

Days fell into a rigorous routine of sample papers. Utsav worked to close the 54-mark gap. As December approached, a new energy buzzed. Republic Day was coming.

"Auditions for Republic Day Cultural Festival - Curricular Activities."

The lists were being made for January 26th: Dancing, Singing, Acting/Drama.

Utsav scanned the circular, his mind racing with the voices and personas he secretly mimicked at home. While Aditi signed up for Debate and Shyam for Volunteer, the stage pulled at Utsav. He wrote his name under Drama. When Aditi asked about his sudden interest, he offered a mysterious smile, joking that since he pretended to understand math every day, acting would be easy.

Gupta Sir sat in the auditorium beside Aadil Bhaiya, the legendary senior who had returned to Ether Enclave to direct the school's

Republic Day performances. They were casting *The Last Letter*, a heavy post-independence drama. When Utsav's turn came, Aadil Bhaiya leaned forward, his charismatic gaze locking onto the younger boy.

"Show me a seventy-year-old broken veteran, Utsav," Aadil instructed softly. "Don't just read the lines. Make me believe the war broke you."

Utsav closed his eyes. When they opened, his youth was gone, replaced by the weary, haunted posture of Captain Vikram. "Mitti ki khushboo wahi hai... lekin log badal gaye hain," his cracked voice echoed across the silent room. He wiped a tear with a trembling hand. "Tiranga sirf ek kapda nahi hai sahab... kafan hai humara."

Pin-drop silence followed. Aditi stopped breathing. Aadil Bhaiya nodded slowly, a proud, knowing smile on his face, and Gupta Sir announced the lead role was his.

The cast list confirmed Aditi as the Journalist and Shyam as Soldier Vijay. Shyam was thrilled until he realized his only job was to die in Utsav's arms. He joked that thinking about Gupta Sir's math class would make dying easy.

Winter rehearsals on the freezing stage were brutal. Utsav struggled with the climax, unable to cry while Shyam played dead by crossing his eyes and sticking his tongue out. Aadil Bhaiya stepped onto the stage, his presence instantly silencing the jokes. He nudged Shyam's leg.

"A soldier doesn't die like a cartoon, Shyam. He dies gasping for his mother," Aadil demonstrated, collapsing with a chilling realism. He turned to Utsav, his eyes fierce. "And you don't just cry, Utsav. You bleed from the inside. When he falls, you aren't losing a co-actor; you are losing a piece of your soul."

When Utsav finally delivered the adjusted monologue, drawing on Aadil's intense coaching, even the cleaning staff stopped to listen. The teachers knew the boy had fire.

The chilling fog eventually gave way to brief, golden afternoons. The group huddled on the cricket mats, sharing peeled oranges, Aditi's homemade *gajar ka halwa*, and endless laughter. Shyam shivered in his thin shirt while Rajat boasted about his imported wool sweater. Utsav silently wrapped his own muffler around Shyam's neck, telling him to save his fire for the stage. He kept the group entertained, chasing Gauri with fake strawberry-flavored blood and flawlessly mimicking the Vice Principal's stiff walk. Aditi watched Utsav run, fast and happy. Shyam noted that Utsav looked good when he smiled, and Aditi agreed. For once, the boy who usually carried the world on his shoulders was just a kid.

On the final rehearsal day, the uniform code was relaxed. Aditi walked in wearing a fitted crimson t-shirt and dark denim, looking like a Bollywood actress. Utsav forgot Captain Vikram completely, staring in absolute awe. She casually announced it was her birthday and opened a steel container of warm, homemade gulab jamuns. Tasting the perfect sweetness, Utsav realized that standing there with her, sharing the laughter of his friends, was a picture far more beautiful than any frame could hold.

January 26, 2014.

The climax arrived on a stage bathed in red light. Gunfire echoed. Shyam ran, took the bullet, and collapsed. Looking down at his friend, Utsav remembered Aadil Bhaiya's words. *Bleed from the inside.* Real tears streamed down Utsav's face. "Mat jao Vijay... Maa ko kya jawab dunga?" His agonizing scream tore through the silent audience. "Kya yahi wo azadi hai... Ki aaj mera bhai yahan sadak pe marega aur koi dekhne wala nahi hoga?"

Aditi paused, visibly moved by his raw intensity, before delivering her final line. The play ended with Utsav saluting the flag in darkness. A thunderous standing ovation followed. The District Magistrate awarded Utsav the Best Actor trophy, declaring that a Class 6 student had taught him the true feeling of patriotism.

Backstage, Shyam hugged him hard, and Aditi whispered that he was perfect. Utsav was no longer just the boy who ranked third; he was the undisputed star of the school. But the applause wasn't the reason for his smile. It was the absolute synchronization he felt with Aditi. The invisible wall between the brilliant top ranker and the quiet boy from West Albizia had vanished. They were partners. He felt he belonged beside her, floating in a golden bubble of perfection where life felt permanently fixed.

But Destiny has a cruel sense of humor. The calmest seas precede the wildest hurricanes. When life feels too good, Fate is quietly arranging a checkmate. Trouble strikes when your guard is down.

Utsav thought his bad days were over. He didn't know the universe balances happiness with a heavy debt of sorrow.

He sat on his roof, flying a kite in the blue sky. He thought about Aditi and the Finals. Life was beautiful.

He didn't see the dark cloud gathering. He was just a boy in love with the world, oblivious that his beautiful glass castle was about to shatter, bringing a pain that would make him wish for his past struggles.

The kite flew higher, unaware that the string was about to snap.

CHAPTER -5

Adyutsav: A Two-Letter Destiny

The Republic Day festivities were over, but the "Party" had just begun. The Chief Guest had handed out cash rewards, and the school didn't deduct a single rupee.

Utsav, Shyam, Zaid, and Kamal sat dividing their share.

"No deduction!" Shyam laughed. "My hard work of dying on stage paid off!" "Dying is an art," Shyam retorted to Zaid's teasing.

Utsav smiled, sipping his Frooti. The world was good. He had money, fame, and the memory of the play.

"Listen!" a voice cut through the laughter. It was Gauri.

Utsav's heart jumped. *Is she calling me?* But Gauri wasn't looking at him.

"Rajat," Gauri said sharply. "Aditi wants to talk to you."

Utsav's smile froze. The Frooti tasted bitter. *If only that voice was for me.*

Rajat didn't look up from his phone. "I don't want to talk to her."

Aditi stepped out from behind Gauri, looking frustrated. "Rajat. Ek baar baat karke dekh lo." (Just talk once).

"Nahi," Rajat snapped, standing up. "Bahut ho chuka. (It's been enough). I don't want to talk to you." He walked away, leaving Aditi upset.

Utsav sat paralyzed. Gauri's sentence looped in his mind, poisoning his blood: *Minute 0: Aditi wants to talk to Rajat.* (Logical: Probably about class work.) *Minute 2: Aditi wants a conversation with Rajat.* (Emotional: Why is the Queen begging for his attention?) *Minute 4: Aditi wants Rajat.* (Insecure: She ignored the whole world just to get two minutes with him.) *Minute 6: Aditi belongs to Rajat.* (Broken: They are connected. I am just the audience clapping in the dark.)

Utsav walked away to a quiet spot under the Neem tree. He remembered Kuldeep Sir's Hindi lecture: "Love means setting someone free."

Utsav scoffed internally. Freedom is for those who have a relationship. For one-sided lovers, there is only the cage of their own thoughts. "If she chooses someone else, I will be happy for her," he had told himself. It was a lie. It burned. Was he a bad person for feeling jealous?

His mind escaped to the summer of 2012. Class 5. Separation from Aditi felt unbearable.

Unable to handle the loneliness, Utsav had torn a piece of paper, writing three initials: *A. K. Y.* He pressed the paper against his chest, wrapping his arms around himself. In the silence, he imagined it was her. He felt the phantom weight of her head on his shoulder, her hands soothing his back. For those few minutes, hugging a scrap of paper under a brick on his terrace, Utsav felt overwhelming peace.

But fear would creep in. *What if someone finds this? Her name will be tarnished.* He would tear the paper and flush it, destroying the proof of his love to protect her honor.

Utsav snapped back to 2014. The memory made his eyes sting. He realized the tragic beauty of Ek Tarfa Pyar (One-Sided Love).

In his imagination, she was his. He was Sikandar (The Conqueror). In reality, he had no Haq (Right). He had no right to stop her from talking to Rajat.

Unrequited love had turned a King into a Pauper. He was just a boy who loved a girl, and sometimes, that was the most painful thing in the world.

Sitting on his terrace, his mind became a Courtroom.

The Lawyer: She ignored you! Does your love mean nothing? *The Judge:* Did he ever confess his feelings? *The Accused:* No, Your Honor. *The Victim:* But I cared for her! I cleaned mud off my pants for her! I became a Topper for her!

Utsav closed his eyes. His love was unilateral. It was his choice to love her. If she loved Rajat, it wasn't her fault. Love cannot be forced. It flows like a river; you cannot build a dam and demand it stay.

A selfish cloud passed over his heart. *I transformed myself into the 'Star of Chronos' to be worthy of her. Where is my return on investment?*

The innocent side fought back. *Did Aditi ever ask you to become a topper? No. You did those things for yourself, using her as the muse.* Utsav realized he was punishing himself for a crime she didn't even know was committed.

To stop his heart from breaking, his brain invented alternative scenarios. *Maybe Aditi sees Rajat as a brother? She wants to tie a Rakhi. Maybe she is a strict businesswoman demanding her Tupperware back because Rajat ate three Gulab Jamuns. Maybe Rajat took a loan for that imported thermal and she wants her 500 Rupees.*

These ridiculous scenarios were the only things keeping him sane. But as the sun set, reality settled.

He had worked hard to become "Unforgettable"—Best Student, Best Actor. He thought excellence was the key to her heart. But he realized a painful truth: You can be the most perfect book in the library, but you cannot force the reader to pick you up.

He was unforgettable to the school, but to her, he was just a classmate. That realization hurt more than any failure. He had conquered the world for her, only to realize she wasn't even watching the war.

Sitting on the edge of his bed, he remembered standing up to the Ojas Enclave bullies to protect Aditi. But today, the threat was a simple sentence: "Aditi wants to talk to Rajat."

The connection of their names felt like acid. How could he show his face to her knowing her eyes searched for someone else?

A desperate urge rose: *Go tell her. You have the words. You are the "Best Actor."*

But paralysis set in. *What will she say? She is looking for Rajat. She might just ask me to move aside.* The system crashed.

Utsav sought refuge in The Geeta. Shri Krishna said: "You have a right to perform your duty, but you are not entitled to the fruits of action."

If he expected her to love him back, it wasn't Love; it was a Business Deal. If he couldn't accept her choices, he was trying to trade affection for obedience. Love wasn't a transaction. He had to love her happiness—even if it meant standing next to Rajat.

If he told his friends, Shyam would laugh, Zaid would analyze, and Rajat would pity him. He couldn't bear pity. He decided to bury it in the deepest dungeon of his heart.

But fear remained: *What if I see them laughing together? The boy in the mirror will say, "You were the King of the Stage, but in your own story, you are just an extra."*

A crushing realization hit him. Silence is dangerous. If you don't tell someone you love them, you cannot blame them for taking a different path. Relationships die in silence. He hadn't even laid the first brick. While he waited for the "Perfect Moment," the moment passed him by, holding Rajat's hand.

One-sided love is safe because no one can reject you, but deadly because no one can accept you.

Utsav stood as the tragic architect of a masterpiece no one ordered. He won every battle, only to find his castle empty. His greatest error was treating affection like a syllabus, calculating that hard work inevitably equaled love. He forgot that love is a lottery of the soul. He was a sealed envelope containing a beautiful letter—destined to sit in a dark drawer, never reaching its address.

February 1, 2014. The School Terrace.

The secret was crushing Utsav. He found Shyam near the water tank.

"Shyam," Utsav whispered. "I need to tell you something. About... Aditi."

Shyam sighed heavily, not turning. "I already knew. I suspected it from the beginning."

Utsav froze. "When? Why didn't you tell me?"

Shyam finally turned, his eyes tired. "What was the point? I was struggling to survive that same pain myself. Until I healed from my own heartbreak, how could I tell you about yours?"

"We both loved her! Shouldn't there have been transparency?" Utsav cracked in desperation.

"It happened," Shyam shrugged. "Let it go."

"She was my first love! How can I forget her?"

"Then go get her! Is she pining for you?" Shyam snapped.

"If you had told me, I would have tried to tell her how I felt," Utsav pleaded.

"And what would you have said? Who are we to question her choice?" Shyam stepped closer. "Is it really love? Have we ever done anything for her? Did you ever... even once... see feelings for yourself in her eyes?"

The words hit like stones. Utsav replayed every memory—the mud incident, rehearsals, the Gulab Jamuns. He saw care and friendship. But he didn't see the specific gaze of longing. She had never looked at him the way he looked at her.

"Brother," Shyam's voice softened. "No human notices love until it is expressed. We were late. And now... she belongs to someone else."

Shyam turned Utsav toward the classroom window. "Look."

Inside, Aditi was laughing genuinely with Rajat. She looked radiant and complete.

"Look at her happiness," Shyam whispered. "Rajat might not be a topper or an actor. But he is her choice. Rajat has won. And we... we have lost."

The image burned into Utsav's retinas. The delusion shattered. *She was never mine. She simply never belonged to me.* Utsav finally accepted the defeat of his first love.

Class 6-A shifted to the grim reality of February. Final Exams approached. Aditi worked harder than ever to be perfect, wanting to shine so bright that Rajat would realize her worth.

But Utsav hung up his armor. The fire to bridge the 54-mark gap, the ambition, the drive to impress her—evaporated. He was tired. *I just want to pass,* he thought. *I just want to go to Class 7 and disappear.*

Utsav began a subconscious campaign of avoidance. He loved her, which was exactly why he couldn't be near her. Every smile was a reminder of his defeat.

The Backbench Silence

Usually, the backbench was a hub of chatter. During a free period, Aditi turned around.

"Utsav," she sought his help. "This date regarding the Mughal Empire..."

In the past, Utsav would have recited the timeline. Today, he pretended to drop his pen, hiding under the desk. "Ask Zaid.

He knows everything," his muffled voice echoed. Aditi looked confused but turned to Zaid.

The Tiffin Break Escape

Lunch break. Aditi opened her box. "I brought Poha."

Utsav stood instantly. "Water," he lied. "I am very thirsty." He spent the entire break staring at a blank washroom wall to avoid sitting where she might look at him.

The Library Seat

In the library, there was one empty chair next to Aditi. He saw her expecting him to sit. He walked past her and sat next to Preeti. Aditi watched him, a flicker of hurt in her eyes. He didn't look back; he couldn't afford to melt.

At home, the playful boy was gone. Trying to erase her only summoned her image. He opened his drawer and found the August School Journal. The photograph: Utsav in the center, Aditi on the left, Ayushi on the right.

"It's a lie," he whispered bitterly. "In this photo, we are together. But in reality, her heart is with Rajat." He hated the captured false closeness. He shoved the journal deep under old newspapers, burying the evidence of his hope.

Exam season arrived. Utsav was revising near the staircase. Aditi walked towards him, radiant and confident, coming to wish him luck.

Panic seized him. If she smiled, the cycle would restart. "Oh no! I forgot my geometry box!" Utsav shouted to no one, sprinting toward the locker room, leaving Aditi with a half-raised wave. He hid behind a pillar, breathing hard.

The final bell of Class 6 rang, echoing across the brick walls of Vidya International School. For six hundred students, that bell was the sweet sound of liberation. It meant sleeping in, endless cricket matches, and freedom from Gupta Sir's math drills.

For Utsav, that bell sounded like a life sentence.

Exams were the only thing that had forced his brain to focus on something other than Aditi. The syllabus was his anchor. Now, the anchor was gone, and he was adrift in a terrifying ocean of free time.

He walked out of the school gates without looking back. He didn't wait near the water cooler. He didn't try to catch a glimpse of her laughing with Rajat. He simply boarded his bus, rested his head against the cool glass window, and made a firm, logical decision.

I am going to move on.

It was a brilliant plan in theory. He was a boy of immense discipline. If he could memorize eight hundred GK questions in a month, surely he could train his brain to forget one girl. He approached heartbreak the way Bhaiya approached a flawed balance sheet: identify the bad asset, write off the loss, and close the ledger.

The Purge The moment he reached his room in West Albizia, Operation Erase began. He emptied his school bag, pulling out the rough notebooks. He flipped through the pages, intending to stack them away for the scrap dealer.

On the very last page of his History notebook, written in tiny, faint pencil strokes hidden in the corner, were three letters: *A. K. Y.* Utsav stared at it. His chest tightened. He grabbed an eraser and scrubbed the letters violently until the paper tore. He threw the notebook into the carton, breathing hard.

Gone. Out of sight, out of mind.

The Betrayal of Habit The theory of "out of sight, out of mind" only works if the mind agrees to cooperate.

Utsav woke up at 6:30 AM automatically. He lay in bed, staring at the ceiling fan. His brain, conditioned by a year of silent devotion, began its daily routine without his permission.

6:30 AM. She is probably waking up now. 7:00 AM. She is braiding her hair. 7:45 AM. She is crossing the Zenith bridge. "Stop it," Utsav whispered aloud, pressing the heels of his hands into his eyes. He forced himself out of bed and went to the terrace to fly his kite. He needed to look at the sky, not the school.

He released the kite, watching it catch the strong March wind. It soared high, a tiny speck of crimson against the vast blue canvas. He smiled. He was doing it. He was enjoying the moment.

Then, the wind shifted. The kite dipped, the crimson paper fluttering gracefully against the breeze.

It looks exactly like the red t-shirt she wore on her birthday during play rehearsals, his traitorous brain whispered.

Utsav's hands went numb. He let go of the spool. The thread unspooled rapidly, and the crimson kite drifted away, lost to the horizon. He sat down on the rough brick wall of the terrace, defeated by a piece of paper.

The Sabotage of the Mundane Moving on is not failing to climb a mountain; it is tripping over a pebble. Aditi was not just a person to him anymore; she had infected his entire vocabulary.

At lunch, his mother served him food. "Utsav, eat properly. I made Karela today."

Utsav looked at the bitter gourd. Instantly, the dining table vanished. He was back in the Class 6-A lunch circle, swapping his delicious paneer for her bitter gourd just to see her smile. He remembered her laughing, calling him a goat.

He took a bite of the Karela. It tasted like ash. He chewed slowly, his eyes watering, forcing it down not out of love, but out of a desperate need to prove it didn't hurt.

That afternoon, he went to the local ground to play cricket with Shyam. "Focus, brother!" Shyam yelled from behind the stumps. "You are batting like you are holding a spoon!"

Utsav grunted, taking his stance. The bowler ran in. A fast, bouncing delivery. Utsav stepped back, calculating the trajectory flawlessly, preparing to pull the ball over the boundary.

Out of the corner of his eye, near the boundary line, a little girl ran past. She was wearing white hair ribbons.

Utsav's focus shattered. The bat slipped in his grip.

Crack. The ball bypassed his edge and smashed directly into his knee. Utsav collapsed onto the dusty pitch, curling into a ball as sharp pain flared up his leg.

Shyam ran over, dropping his keeping gloves. "Utsav! Are you crazy? You didn't even swing! Where were you looking?"

Utsav lay in the dust, clutching his knee, but he wasn't crying because of the physical pain. He was crying because he realized the terrifying truth. He couldn't hide from her. She wasn't just in the school; she was in the wind, in the food, in the white ribbons of strangers.

"I can't do it, Shyam," Utsav whispered into the dirt, his voice cracking. "I try not to think about her, but it takes all my energy just to pretend I'm not thinking about her. And then I end up thinking about her anyway."

Shyam sighed, kneeling in the dust beside his best friend. He didn't offer a joke. He just patted Utsav’s back. "You can't delete a file if the system is still running the program, bhai. Stop fighting it. Let it hurt. Eventually, it will get tired."

The Birth of the Echo By the second week of the holidays, Utsav stopped fighting.

He realized that actively trying to forget Aditi was like trying to hold his breath—eventually, his lungs would burn, and he would have to gasp for her memory just to survive.

So, sitting alone in his room as the warm Chronos evening settled outside, Utsav made a dangerous psychological compromise. A compromise that would shape the next ten years of his life.

If the *Real Aditi* belonged to Rajat, and the real world was too painful to inhabit... he would simply create a world where she belonged to him.

He closed his eyes. He didn't picture the Aditi who looked at Rajat. He pictured the Aditi who had washed the mud off his knee. The Aditi who had clapped for him when he recited poetry. The Aditi who had offered him warm gulab jamuns.

In the silence of his room, he imagined her sitting on the edge of his bed. *Why are you so sad?* his mind projected her voice—sweet, pure, and entirely focused on him. *Because I lost you,* Utsav thought back. *You didn't lose me. I am right here.*

Utsav opened his eyes. The room was empty. But the heavy, suffocating pain in his chest had miraculously lightened. The

Real Aditi was miles away, living her own life. But the Imaginary Aditi had just moved in.

He didn't realize it then, but Utsav was laying the foundation bricks for the "Silent Decade." He was building a pristine, unbreakable glass castle inside his own mind, where he could be the King, and she would always be the Queen.

The final verdict was pasted on the notice board. Rank 1: Aditi. Untouchable. Rank 2: Gauri. Rank 3: Ayushi.

And Utsav? The "Best Actor," the "Genius of West Albizia"—was nowhere on the leaderboard. Not even in the Top 5. He had successfully faded into the average crowd.

He watched Aditi celebrate from a distance. He felt relief. He didn't want his name associated with hers. He walked away, heart strangely empty. He had lost the academic race, but protected his heart. Or so he thought.

Walking out of the gates, he realized running away had only cemented her presence in his soul. He had nowhere to go but inward, where she lived rent-free.

The espresso machine sliced through the silence at Starbucks. Sumit stopped speaking. The story of Utsav hung in the air.

Aarohi sat frozen, processing a Class 6 heartbreak that sounded terrifyingly adult.

"So..." she trembled. "He just... gave up? Walked away?"

"He didn't walk away," Sumit corrected gently. "He faded away. Fading away happens when you have no fight left."

Aarohi looked up, frustration creeping in. "But why? She cleaned mud off his pants! Why didn't he just tell her?"

Sumit smiled a sad, knowing smile. "Because Utsav believed if you love someone, you don't burden them. He thought telling Aditi would ruin her happiness with Rajat. He thought his silence was a gift."

"That's stupid. That’s self-sabotage."

"Is it? Or is it the purest form of respect? To value someone's choice more than your desire?"

Aarohi shook her head violently. "No. It’s fear. He was scared of rejection."

"Aarohi, Utsav’s tragedy wasn't just the dramatic moments. The real tragedy was in the comedy. Moments the class found hilarious were pure devotion."

The "Karela" Conspiracy (November 2013)

"Oh no! Mom packed Karela!" Aditi groaned at lunch.

"Eww. I brought Maggi. I am not sharing," Rajat sneered.

Utsav despised bitter gourd, but he saw Aditi’s sad eyes. "Is that Karela? That’s my favorite! It sharpens the brain. Give it to me."

He swapped his delicious Paneer for her Karela. He forced it down.

"Bhai, you look like you are chewing a rubber tyre dipped in acid," Shyam whispered. "It tastes like... love," Utsav’s eyes watered.

Aditi laughed. "You are so weird! You have the taste buds of a goat!"

The Tragedy: Aditi thought he was weird. She didn't realize a boy who eats bitterness to see you eat sweetness is a keeper.

She traded a "Paneer-Hearted Boy" for a "Maggi-Minded Guy."

The "Ghost" Notebook (December 2013)

Gupta Sir was checking homework. Aditi froze. "I left my Maths notebook at home." Being Rank 1, standing outside was ultimate humiliation.

Utsav silently slid his completed notebook to her. "Scratch my name. Write yours."

"But what about you?"

"I... I like fresh air."

Gupta Sir checked Aditi's book. "Good." He looked at Utsav. "Notebook?"

"Sir... the dog ate it."

"Get out! Stand outside with your hands up!"

The Tragedy: Utsav stood outside for 40 minutes smiling at a lizard so Aditi could be safe. After class, Aditi giggled, "You are a Duffer! Worst excuse ever!" She didn't see the "Protector." She thought it was funny, not realizing only one person ever volunteered to stand in the sun so she could sit in the shade.

The Spider-Man Reflex (January 2014)

A large hairy spider dropped onto Aditi's desk in the library. She screamed. The Zenith Group ran. Rajat jumped back. "Eww! Keep it away!"

Utsav calmly walked over, picked it up with paper, and released it outside. "Go home, Peter Parker."

"Weren't you scared?" Aditi breathed hard.

"It was just a spider."

"I bet you were screaming inside. Are your hands shaking?" She grabbed his hands. They were steady.

The Tragedy: Aditi laughed it off as him trying to be cool. She failed to notice Rajat backed away, while Utsav stepped forward. She let go of the hand that was steady in the face of fear—the hand that would have removed every problem from her life without asking for credit.

"You see, Aarohi?" Sumit said. "Utsav wasn't weak. But poor Aditi. She had a boy who ate bitterness, stood in punishment, and faced fears for her. And she thought he was just a 'funny friend.' One day, she will be eating a bitter meal, and she will look for Rajat... and maybe he won't care. The taste of Karela will come back. She will realize she lost the only person who loved her more than he loved himself. That regret will be heavier than any school bag."

The ghost of Utsav lingered in the car. Aarohi traced the steering wheel. "He was an idiot," she whispered.

"An epic saga, and your verdict is 'Idiot'?" Sumit chuckled.

"A beautiful idiot," she corrected, eyes soft with admiration. "He was pure. Utsav was giving everything for zero return. That's divine."

"It was One-Sided. It doesn't count."

"It counts the most! Aditi is the unluckiest girl. She had a diamond and threw it away for a shiny pebble. Finding a guy who stands outside a class for you? That doesn't happen in real life. Real life is full of Rajats."

Aarohi looked intensely at Sumit. "What happened to him? Did he survive?"

Sumit's warmth faded into a cynical glint. "Survive? Oh, he did more than survive. He killed the Saint. The innocent boy died that summer."

"Who replaced him?"

"A Sinner. He realized if you can't get Love, you should get Everything Else. The new Utsav... is obscenely rich. He has Generational Wealth. And a philosophy."

"What philosophy?"

"That Love is a scam. He chases the high. He treats relationships like a rental car—drive fast, have fun, never park it in your garage."

"So... he's empty? A player?"

"He is Safe. He built a wall so high no girl can climb it. He gives them gifts and time, but never his vulnerability. He'd rather be the Heartbreaker than the Heartbroken."

Aarohi sighed. "That's even sadder. The boy who felt everything now feels nothing."

"He prefers it," Sumit looked out the window.

Aarohi drove, digesting the transformation. "His mistake wasn't loving her. It was waiting for the perfect world. Sometimes... the girl is already stuck in a story she can't write herself out of."

Sumit chose to interpret her words as general philosophy, staying in the happy bubble of Chapter 1.

Later, sitting in Starbucks as the sun set, the story demanded an autopsy.

"He wasn't a boy," Aarohi shook her head. "He was a myth. Bankrupting his dignity to see her smile. He was terrifyingly pure."

"He didn't see it as sacrifice," Sumit said.

"I feel pity for Aditi. She was blind," Aarohi said passionately. "Mark my words. One day, life will serve her a 'Bitter Gourd' moment. She will wait for someone to swap plates. And they won't. She will realize she threw away the only person who truly loved her."

Sumit nodded. "At least Shyam knew."

"Did he? Shyam didn't know Utsav deliberately withdrew from the competition to save her ego. He was suffering in a silence so deep even his best friend couldn't hear the scream. He deserves to be selfish now."

Aarohi checked her watch. "We should go."

As they walked out, the story felt like a heavy coat removed. But for Aarohi, the warning was clear: *Don't be Aditi. Don't miss the diamond.* Yet another voice whispered: *But what if I am already stuck with a pebble I can't throw away?*

She glanced at Sumit, hiding her tragedy behind a smile.

Sumit unlocked his car. Aarohi hesitated. "Did he spend the rest of his life crying? Did he become a monk?"

Sumit chuckled low. "A monk? You are underestimating him like Aditi did. The story of the Real Utsav starts when he walked away from that notice board. He gave up on *her* competition. But survival? He mastered that."

Sumit leaned against the car, painting a picture of glamour. "Destiny handed him keys to a vault. He doesn't eat bitter gourd; he eats at 5-star tables. He doesn't stand outside classrooms; he owns the buildings. He became an Atheist of Romance. He chases dopamine in bottles and fast cars. He is a Mirror—giving girls what they want, but ghosting them if they ask for his heart."

"He became the very thing he hated," Aarohi sat back.

"He became Safe. The new Utsav is the life of the party, but untouchable. He built a fortress of gold so high the memory of a girl in a yellow raincoat could never climb it. He is a magnificent sinner."

"Will I ever meet him?" Aarohi asked playfully.

"Maybe. If you are lucky. Or unlucky. See you, Aarohi."

The streetlights of the city bled into long, golden streaks across the car's windshield. Sumit kept his eyes on the road, his hands relaxed on the steering wheel, while Arohi watched the passing headlights, the heavy silence of the Starbucks conversation still lingering between them.

"I just can't wrap my head around her," Arohi said suddenly, her voice cutting through the soft hum of the engine. "Aditi, I mean. How could she not feel it? You were literally bleeding yourself dry to build a perfect world for her."

Sumit shifted gears, a faint, nostalgic smile touching his lips. "You can't blame someone for not reading a letter you never sent, Arohi. She wasn't blind. She was just looking in a different direction. Rajat was loud. He was a whisper."

"But a whisper that cleared her path," Arohi argued, turning in her seat to look at his profile. "It frustrates me, Sumit. It frustrates me that Utsav thought his silence was this grand, noble sacrifice. It wasn't. It was a tragedy. She traded a boy who would have moved mountains for a guy who couldn't even connect a physics wire without complaining about his sweater."

"That is the irony of adolescence," Sumit replied smoothly, the brake lights painting his face in a soft red glow. "We fall for the packaging, not the product. Rajat was a shiny, imported box. Utsav was just a heavy, unpolished stone. But you know what the funniest part is?"

"What?"

"If he had confessed back then, it might have ruined the purity of it. The unrequited nature of that love is what forged him. It made him resilient. It taught him how to give without demanding a receipt. If Aditi had chosen him in Class 6, he wouldn't be the man sitting next to Divya."

Arohi softened, looking down at her hands. "So, he forgive her? For choosing Rajat?"

"There is nothing to forgive," Sumit said quietly, glancing at her with an absolute, grounding certainty. "She was a chapter he had to read to understand the rest of the book. She was the draft. You, Arohi... you are the published manuscript."

Arohi smiled, gently leaning her tired head against the cool, tinted glass of the passenger window. The ghost of Aditi finally stopped haunting the quiet car, left far behind in the rearview mirror.

सौभाग्यशाली वे हैं, या दुर्भाग्य हमारा है

जसिकी ख़ातरि मंदरिों में, शीश मैंने था झुकाया, बनि गुज़ारशि ही कसिी ने, सहजता से उसे पाया।
माँगता था मन्नत, बाँध कर धागे हज़ारों में, क्या कमी थी मेरी नष्ठिा, या मेरी करुण पुकारों में?

जसिकी चाहत में भुला दी, ज़दिगी की हर डगर, बनि तलब के ही कसिी के, बन गए वो हमसफ़र।
स्वप्न सारे राख कर के, बस उसी को था सँवारा, और उसने अजनबी को, चुन लयिा अपना कनिारा।

मैं अभागा बस मलिन की, तैयारयिों में रह गया, वो बड़ी आसानी से ही, और की नदयिा बह गया।
मैं सजाता ही रहा था, ख़्वाब की वो थालयिाँ, ले गया कोई चुरा कर, मेरे बाग की डालयिाँ।

मैं तड़प कर रो रहा था, आंसुओं की धार में, वो खलिौना बन गया है, अब कसिी के प्यार में।
चीख़ती रह गई मेरी, आशकि़ी उस मोड़ पर, चल दएि वो अश्क मेरे, बीच में ही छोड़ कर।

मेरे सच्चे प्रेम को, कर के यकायक नज़रंदाज़, मलि गया वो और को, है यह नयिति का कैसा राज़!
इश्क़ की इस आज़माइश में, हार मेरी हो गई, आँख के सम्मुख ही मेरी, जान मेरी खो गई।

THE END

www.ingramcontent.com/pod-product-compliance
Ingram Content Group UK Ltd.
Pitfield, Milton Keynes, MK11 3LW, UK
UKHW040034200726
13845UKWH00053B/256

9 789357 777971